A

BLACKENED

HEART

A Willow Green Village Cozy Mystery

Evelyn Harrison

Raven Crest Books

Copyright © 2016 Evelyn Harrison

Cover Design by www.StunningBookCovers.com

ISBN: 978-0-9934439-5-4

This book is dedicated to everyone whose lives have been touched by cancer. My own parents, Fred and Jean, both died of the decease. Dad died first, in 1966 from pancreatic cancer and my mum in 1995 from ovarian cancer. Even after all these years, these cancers are still causing devastation to families, mainly because symptoms go undetected and diagnosis comes too late for successful treatment. I pray that in the not too distant future, for all our sakes, this will not continue to be the case.

PART 1

CHAPTER 1 – THE MANUSCRIPT

It was now or never. Pat Wood looked up towards the clock over her mantelpiece as it began to strike eight o'clock. The old Victorian timepiece had sat majestically above the fireplace, in Honeysuckle Cottage, ever since she had purchased it, almost twenty years ago, from a jumble sale in Willow Green Village Hall. It was the kind of clock you had to wind religiously every day, but she didn't mind that, the sound of its continuous ticking was somehow confirmation that she was still breathing, still alive. It had been over a week now since she finally finished her manuscript. Some people say there is a book in every one of us; certainly in Pat's case it was true and its creation had been a long time coming. She had begun writing it years ago, putting pen to paper, crossing out and rewriting. To be frank, progress had been slow, until the day she decided to splash out and buy a laptop. Not the top of the range kind – no, on her pension she couldn't afford one of those – just a cheap one, a 'manager's special,' good enough for the job. Now the book was complete and waiting patiently on her sideboard, taking up the space where a vase of flowers would normally sit, waiting for someone else to read it. That someone, she had decided, would be her neighbour, Josie Forrester.

She had resided next door to the Forrester family ever since she moved to Willow Green, watching with fondness as their little family had grown and prospered. Then, with some sadness, as one by one their daughters, Beth and Emma, had left home to embark on lives of their own. Josie could always rely on her to feed Sandy, their ginger tom, when they went on holiday, or take in parcels too big for the letterbox, or even let in the electricity man when he came to read the meter. Yes, Pat was a good neighbour, but, when the curtains were drawn and the only company she had were her memories, well, she was a very lonely one, too.

As the minute hand moved to five past the hour, Pat gathered up her folder and, closing her front door behind her, she hobbled to the end of her flower-bordered path, turned immediate left and clicked open the little wooden gate leading up to Brook Cottage. Walking through the arch at the side of the red brick building, she knocked on the back door and was immediately greeted by Josie.

"Morning Pat, how are you?" Josie asked, peering at her neighbour through her morning eyes, "I have to say you're still looking a little under the weather. Did you see the doctor like I suggested?" she added, concerned about her friend's pallid complexion.

Pat smiled, the sort of smile that said, 'Thanks for the concern' – although Josie could not help but notice she avoided eye contact with her as she began her reply.

"Yes, he said there's not much to worry about. I'm fine really, just a bit run down. It's simply old age catching up with me. Josie, the reason I came round … I've written a book and I wanted to ask a big favour. Would you read it for me and tell me what you think?" she requested, just as her hand reached into the thin plastic carrier bag she had been clutching at her side.

Josie looked slightly taken aback by her question. "You're a dark horse, Pat. Wow, a book."

Pat removed the manuscript from her bag and laid it carefully on the kitchen table. Josie realised there was no getting out of reading it now without looking a complete shit.

"You do understand I'm a maths teacher not an English teacher," she pointed out, "I mean, if you want it edited or something?"

Pat grinned. "I would just like you to read it. I consider you a dear friend, and I trust your judgement. Please, just peruse it for me and tell me what you think. That's all."

Josie started to flick through the pages. "So, I'm curious, is it about the good folk of Willow Green? Are you about to upset the villagers?"

"No, I wouldn't dare do that, I have to live here. Although … I must admit I've been privy to quite a few unsavoury stories which would make even the most worldly of people blush." Pat pulled out a chair and eased herself onto the seat. "I used to live in Wareford, a small town in Hertfordshire, and I've based my story around acquaintances I made there. I've been writing it for ages and now I have finally finished it. I won't spoil it for you, but I'm hoping you'll be surprised by the story line. I've even included a few murders," she enticed.

"Do you think your 'acquaintances' from Wareford will be upset?"

"Perhaps, I'll know soon enough; I've sent a copy to a friend of mine who still lives there."

"I see. Well, as it happens, Max is going to be away on a boys' only weekend with Richard – you know, my friend Linda's husband – so, over the next couple of days, I could give it my undivided attention."

Pat rose carefully to her feet, stifling the urge to cry out at the intense pain now shooting through her body. She had hated lying to Josie, but the results from her tests at the hospital were not good. Doctor O'Brien had been very gentle and had spoken slowly so she could absorb the shattering words no one wants to hear. Two months till the end of her life is all he gave her. Two months in a hospital bed, surrounded by strangers, being kept alive in a state of semi-consciousness by hallucinogenic drugs.

She recalled the parcel she received in yesterday's post, an early birthday present from an old friend. Yes, she would go back to her little cottage, open the welcome package and enjoy the sweetness from the little golden nuggets of confectionary with a nice cup of tea. Leaving her precious work in Josie's hands, she succumbed to the feeling of finality.

***

Much later that same day, before Josie had a chance to begin her committed task, the tune from her iPad brought her temporarily out of her self-induced gloom, as she returned the smile of her youngest daughter now visible to her on FaceTime.

"Hi Mum, I know Dad's away, wondered if you'd like to come up to the farm? Kate and her spiritualist group are coming round, we're going to have a circle," Beth enthused.

Josie sighed, how she would have enjoyed an evening with her daughter, but no, a promise was a promise.

"Would have loved to, darling. Kate's becoming quite infamous around here with her psychic abilities, but Pat was here this morning with a manuscript, of all things, and I've given her my word I'd read it this weekend. Sorry."

"Really? What sort of book has Aunty Pat written?"

Beth had called Pat 'Aunty Pat' ever since she was a little girl, and, to be truthful, Pat loved the feeling of warmth it still brought her.

"It's a novel, based in a town she used to live, apparently. She gave me the impression it's a thriller, you never know it might be a bit saucy too, but perhaps that's just wishful thinking on my part. I guess she thought she would try her hand at writing when she retired from the teashop. "

"Good for her."

"My thoughts exactly. Look, give my love to Kate. Perhaps I'll join you all next time."

Josie ended her call and poured herself a large glass of white wine. Opening the folder, she began to read.

PART 2

CHAPTER 2 – MARY MACEY

What on earth did I do in my past that fate decided I was due for a good kicking? I definitely believe in fate, believe we all begin life with a destiny, but sometimes, misguidedly or not, we take the wrong turning and embark on the wrong road. Where did my fateful journey begin into this deep, dark chasm from which I'm only just emerging? My childhood was a happy one, mum, dad, brother ... yes, I think it began with my darling brother.

***

"Are you sure you've packed enough clothes, Teddy? You are going for a fortnight you know, you must have changed at least three times yesterday, not that I was counting," I mocked, as my brother Edward (known to everyone as Teddy) crammed yet another pair of lurid shorts into his bulging suitcase.

Oblivious to my sarcasm, he thought seriously for a minute. "Do you think I should take another couple of t-shirts, Mary? Only Steve said we'll be partying most nights, if he has anything to do with it."

He and Steven Maddox had been best mates since primary school, and Steve had always been around to protect Teddy from the bullies in the playground, who sadly thought my curly-haired, grey-eyed, delicately featured brother was an easy target for their mindless games. Over the past few years, Steve and his parents had taken their vacations in the United States. However, this year, because the two friends had finished their A levels and were going off in separate directions to their respective colleges, Steve had persuaded his parents to let Teddy join them. I had to admit when my brother first told me of his trip I was more than a little envious – Miami, Florida still being an exotic destination at the beginning of the seventies.

"Honestly, Teddy, you have more than enough and anyway, this might come as a surprise to you, but they do have shops out there – I'm sure you'll be tempted to buy one or two things."

"Ok, little sis, you're right as always. I'm going to miss your bossiness, you know." He reached into his back pocket and took out his wallet. "Look, I've put a picture of you in here, so it's like you're coming with me." He grinned at seeing my face light up at this disclosure, before finally snapping his case shut for the last time, just as the front doorbell rang.

"They're here," Ruth, our mum, called urgently from the bottom of the stairs, "hurry up Teddy, you mustn't keep Mr and Mrs Maddox waiting."

While Mr Maddox, an austere looking gentleman with a well-groomed handlebar moustache, tied Teddy's suitcase securely to the roof of his pride and joy, a 1969 Rover Saloon, Teddy quickly kissed us goodbye, before jumping into the back seat next to Steve.

"Bye, have fun, don't forget to send a postcard," Mum bellowed, as Mr Maddox turned the ignition key, starting the powerful engine. We both watched tearfully as the car roared away down the street, before finally disappearing out of our sight.

"Don't worry Mum, they'll be fine," I coaxed, my arm encircling her shoulders, trying to pacify her as she sobbed into her sodden hanky.

"I'm sure they will, but Teddy … well, Teddy has always been special. You know what I mean, Mary?"

Yes, I knew what my mum meant. She did not have to say any more, sexuality being a taboo subject for discussion at that time. All the same, Teddy was the kindest and most caring brother anyone could ever have; talk of his sexual preferences was never debated, because, quite frankly, it made no difference to the love we all felt towards him and nor should it have done.

"Well," she sighed, finally pulling herself together, "I'd better get back to the bakery, your dad will be wondering where I am."

Mum and my dad, George, a quiet unassuming man who irrefutably was going a little thin on top, had built up quite a reputation over the years for having the most delicious breads and cakes found anywhere within a two-mile radius. The smell of warm, baked bread wafting from our shop, aptly called Macey's Bakery, was always a welcoming enticement for the locals of our small Hertfordshire town of Wareford.

When my parents first purchased the establishment, they had lived in the one bed flat above, but, after my brother and I came along, Mum had managed to persuade Dad to spend some of his hard-earned money on a detached house on the edge of town. She soon discovered she was in her element, mainly due to the acre of land that came with the property, enabling her to have ducks and chickens, alongside an impressive vegetable garden.

"Mary, collect the eggs will you?" she asked, running a comb through her tightly permed hair, before putting on her blue overalls, with the name 'Macey's Bakery' clearly embossed in gold. "Only, I didn't have time this morning. Is Violet coming around today?"

"Yes, she said she'd be along later."

Violet Bell was my best friend and an unquestionable flirt. Her bottle bleached hair and baby blue eyes inevitably made her a magnet to the male population. She was the youngest of three sisters and her father, Paddy, a larger than life character with a booming voice, was the landlord of The Crown public house. I believe that Violet's flirtatious and – on many an occasion – embarrassing behaviour where boys were concerned, was the consequence of being raised in such a social environment.

I had my head in the hen house when Violet, dressed in hot pants and long white boots, called round for me.

"Christ, Mare, is that chicken shit on your trainers?" Looking down at my feet, I began to scrape the offending mess off onto the grass. Trying hard to conceal her disgust, Violet continued. "Did Teddy get off ok with that gorgeous Steve Maddox? Talk about tall, dark, and handsome, ooh he's so yummy."

I tried to ignore her last remark before replying. "Yes, they should just about be at the airport by now."

"Come on then, Mare, put your glad rags on. I'm taking you for a burger down at that new place; the gang are already down there celebrating our liberation from school."

The 'gang' were mostly made up of Violet's female hangers-on, who worshipped her as a goddess of fashion.

Still trying to clean off my trainers before going back into the house, I grumbled, "Wish you'd stop it about Steve, you know it makes me feel uncomfortable. You just have to accept he's not interested in you."

I brought to mind last year's Christmas party at The Crown, when, because we had both reached the age of sixteen, Violet's father had allowed us to join in the festivities. Unbeknown to him, though, Violet had sneaked a half bottle of vodka in her handbag and was adding it to her lemonade throughout the evening. In her intoxicated state, she had approached Steve as he emerged from the men's toilets, offering to show him her 'lady bits'. He declined the offer (I would like to believe because he is a gentleman) and made his exit quickly from the pub. Violet – not one for giving up – had run outside after him, before she unceremoniously slipped on the iced-covered pavement and chipped one of her front teeth as her face hit the hard surface. The aftermath of her fall had meant several trips to the dentist as well as a dented ego.

Sadly, a deluded Violet still believed she stood a chance with Steve. "I'll win him round, you mark my words: Steve Maddox will be mine one day. I will just have to work out which buttons to press, if you know what I mean."

Exasperated by my friend's continuing fantasy, I

smiled weakly and went in to change.

***

Ten long days later, a postcard with a picture of a white sandy beach and palm trees at last arrived from Teddy.

Hi All,

Having a fab time, it's really hot and humid here. Hotel is out of this world. Spending most of our days on the beach or in the pool, where Steve has been flexing his muscles. Americans are really friendly. Meals are enormous must of put on at least ten pounds already. Mary, have been shopping, might have even bought you a little something.

Miss you, all my love, Teddy xxx

Mum read it repeatedly for the next few days, to anyone and everyone who was unfortunate to be in earshot.

"Ok Ruth, I think you've just about read it to the entire town now, enough is enough and anyway he'll be home in three days."

Dad sighed as he turned the 'Open' sign on the bakery door. He loved his son but, if he were honest, he deeply regretted he had never shown any interest in the family business. He remembered his heartache the day Teddy told them he wanted to go to college to study interior design.

"What sort of job is that for a man?" he had argued, in the strongest possible terms.

Over time, mum managed to persuade him to support their cherished son but, all the same, it was obviously still a big disappointment to him.

Saturday dawned and Mum was already busy cooking Teddy's favourite meal, when the Maddox's Rover drew up in front of our house and Teddy, looking tanned but tired, in Bermuda shorts and a yellow t-shirt with the word 'Miami' running diagonally across it, emerged from the vehicle. Both of us rushed eagerly to greet him; anyone watching would have thought he had been away for years, not two weeks, the way we carried on.

"Tell us all about it; you know we only got one post card from you," Mum cried enthusiastically, almost before he had time to get through the door.

"Mum, if you don't mind, we've been travelling for more than twelve hours – can we talk later? I really could do with a bath and a sleep right now, if that's ok." Trying not to show her frustration, she conceded he did actually look exhausted. Taking me by the hand, he coaxed, "Come up with me, Mary, I want to show you the things I've brought back."

Up in his bedroom, Teddy opened his suitcase and commenced spreading the contents all over his bed.

"I knew it! Look at all your new clothes, how the hell did you get the case shut?" I laughed. He grinned before handing me a neatly wrapped parcel. Squealing with delight, I held aloft two fashionable tops. "Wow, Violet will be jealous, thanks; thanks a lot Teddy," I cried, hugging him tightly. "Did you have a good time then? I can't tell you how much I've missed having you around."

"The best ever – even made a friend, Joe, the son of the hotel owner, we seemed to jell instantly; he spent a lot of time showing us all the best places to hang out. Steve didn't care for him much though, thought he was too full of himself, but he and I really got on, he even promised he would keep in touch."

"I'm glad you made a new friend. Well, I'd better let you get some rest."

"Before you go sis, I must own up to a couple of things. First, I'm sorry, but I lost your picture, I did search everywhere for it, but it just disappeared. The other thing ... Steve didn't stop talking about you while we were away; I think he might even have a bit of a crush." I found this revelation a bit hard to believe.

"I'm sure you've got that wrong. Anyway, Violet's still hung up on him, swear you'll never mention this in front of her."

"Whatever you say. My lips are sealed."

"As for the picture, well it's actually quite exciting to think an image of me is on the other side of the Atlantic."

From that day on, I did my best to keep my distance from Steve; making up any lame excuse for being out when he came round. The last thing I wanted was to fall out with my best friend.

***

By the end of September, Teddy had begun his college course and I was working alongside our parents in the bakery. Several years before, I had been diagnosed with asthma and the very sight of a cloud of flour dust sent me off into a wheezing fit. The little pink pills our doctor had prescribed definitely helped, but I hated their disturbing side effects. The minute they slid down my throat, my heart seemed to pound louder and more rapidly, almost as if it was trying to get out of my chest – a particularly alarming scenario – as I lay in bed at night. Because of my condition, I was not able to get involved, in any shape or form, with bread or cake making, so was forced to accept the position of serving the customers besides Mum, which I actually quite enjoyed. I could tell it had been a great relief to Dad when I exhibited interest in learning about the family business and, for the time being at least, life in the Macey household was jogging along nicely.

Of course, my good intention to keep away from Steve proved more difficult as the weeks went by. Then, one evening, as I was making my weary way home, a figure emerged from the shadows.

"I think you've been avoiding me Mary Macey, now why is that?" Steve began, putting a light to his cigarette. Troubled by his appearance, I began to walk faster. "Slow down, I just want to talk to you. How about I treat you to a drink?" Counting out the money in his hand, he added, "I could even stretch to a plate of chips, if you're hungry?" It was obvious he was not going to take 'no' for an answer and reluctantly I followed him into a nearby cafe. "So, where have you been hiding? I've not seen you for ages." I lowered my eyes.

"Teddy told me he thought you fancied me. I know that sounds silly," I said, cringing with embarrassment as the words left my mouth.

"Well, what if I do? You're very beautiful you know. I've always had a weakness for dark hair and hazel eyes." His gaze seemed to bore into me, making me blush. With his left hand, he gently brushed a stray strand of hair away from my face, making me feel even more uncomfortable than I already was.

"Please don't," I said, pushing his hand away. "You know full well that Violet has a crush on you, and as she's my best friend ..."

"I'm off limits. Is that what you're trying to tell me? Look, I have never had, and will never have, any feelings for Violet; she's just a silly little flirt as far as I'm concerned. You, on the other hand, Miss Mary Macey, are wonderful and I would really love to take you out."

I jumped to my feet.

"I'm sorry Steve but, as I said, Violet is my friend," and with that I rushed from the cafe, resisting the urge to look back at the young man who had just made my heart race.

CHAPTER 3 – A VISITOR

Joe Carter was as good as his word. The following month, the first of many letters arrived from Florida and, over the next year, he and Teddy corresponded regularly. I looked forward to reading his mail as much as Teddy did, and through the contents, I was beginning to feel I was getting to know the American reasonably well. Then, one morning, a letter arrived to say his father was sending him to Europe to study hotel management and he would love to take time out to visit us. He went on to explain that we need not worry about putting him up, because his father had contacts locally and he would be staying at one of their hotels for the duration.

Several weeks later, with mounting anticipation, Teddy and I arrived at the entrance to Heathrow Airport. I had never been in an airport before and I was totally in awe. The whole building was pulsating with excitement; thousands of travellers were milling here and there, eager to depart for the numerous destinations around the world. With plenty of time to spare before Joe's plane was expected, we decided to grab a drink and a sandwich.

"Can't wait to see Joe again, you know he is my first real friend, if you know what I mean."

I looked at him, almost choking on my food, before replying in a whisper, "Did I just understand you correctly; were you just admitting to me you're ..." I glanced about me quickly before uttering the next word, "gay?" Teddy looked uneasy.

"Yes, I think I was. Does it bother you?"

I jumped up and threw my arms around him.

"Bother me? No, it's a relief you've finally found the strength to tell me, but you could have chosen a less crowded place to do it. I love you, you silly thing, and always will and if Joe makes you happy, then that's all I care about. I must admit though, his letters never gave me the impression he was that way inclined towards you, but you know him better than I do."

"We didn't actually have a holiday romance or anything; I just felt this connection between us ... I only hope he feels the same way."

Moments later, we were waiting with other interested parties at the barrier, straining hard for the first glimpse of the arrivals off the plane from the United States. I really hoped I was going to like this acquaintance of my brother, who seemed to have had the capability of stealing his heart. It was at that point I happened to notice a large sign, being held aloft by a smartly dressed chauffeur, with the name Joe Carter clearly written in capital letters.

I nudged Teddy. "Looks like we're not the only ones waiting for Joe; his father must have organised a lift."

Focusing now on the approaching passengers, Teddy let out a whoop as he caught sight of a familiar figure. Dressed from head to toe in blue denim and wearing a particularly fetching pair of dark glasses, a broad-shouldered, strikingly attractive young man with sun-bleached hair was now striding purposefully towards us. A rather impressive camera hung around his neck and, as he reached us, he raised it up to eye level and began clicking zealously.

"Joe, wow, it's great to see you again! This is Mary, my sister."

Letting his camera fall once again to his chest, Joe turned to me, an enormous grin erupting across his handsome face.

"You're exactly as Teddy described you. Look, I hope you didn't mind me taking your picture, only photography is a bit of a passion of mine," Joe exclaimed, in his unmistakable American accent, before taking hold of my right hand and kissing it softly, while his eyes rose up towards me. Taken aback by his display of friendliness in front of my brother, I giggled uncomfortably.

Suddenly spotting the sign with his name on it, Joe approached the smartly-suited chauffeur, who turned out to be at his disposal for the entire week. We felt very grand when the dark blue limousine dropped us off outside our house and, from the confines of the car, I could not help but notice a few curious faces at our neighbours' windows. Before we alighted from the vehicle, however, Joe invited us both to dine with him that evening, adding that he would send the car back to collect us.

***

The instant we walked through the revolving door of the five star hotel, the staff greeted us like royalty and immediately showed us up to Joe's luxurious suite of rooms. I felt we had just stepped into a Hollywood film set; never before had I seen a room decorated with such glamour. Floor-length curtains draped the windows, a deep piled white shag carpet covered the floor, and two large red leather settees faced the biggest television screen I had ever seen.

"So glad you both came, come on in. Can I get you a drink? The bar seems to have everything," Joe enthused as he reached for three glasses. "Vodka and coke alright for you, Teddy? What about you Mary? Let me see, you look like someone who enjoys a glass of white wine?" Feeling for the moment like a silly schoolgirl, I grinned at his assumption. "Look, I hope it's ok with you both, but I've arranged to have dinner brought up here. I have to admit, I'm whacked, don't really feel in the mood for putting on a show for the minions downstairs."

I was a little troubled by his use of the word 'minions' but, on the other hand, how could we have any objections to his suggestion? After all, we were his guests.

The meal that followed was a gourmet triumph, which Joe appeared to take for granted – giving no word of thanks to the poor waiter, who seemed more than a little nervous in his presence. This attitude towards the staff was beginning to irritate me a little; I found it hard to believe that Teddy was oblivious to his continuing brusque manner.

"How's Steve, by the way? I must admit, I was slightly disappointed he couldn't come tonight," Joe asked, reclining on one of the settees.

What was Teddy to say? Of course, he had mentioned Joe's visit to Steve and then the invitation to dinner, but all he got from him was: 'The psycho's your friend, not mine'.

"Steve had a prior engagement, new girlfriend apparently." This was not far from the truth, it appeared Steve had finally given up on me and had turned his attentions elsewhere. "So," Teddy began, deliberately changing the subject, "your father got his way then, bringing you into the business?"

I could not help but notice the expression on Joe's face had changed dramatically, and his subsequent words sounded almost venomous. His eyes looked wildly around him as he rose to his feet and began pacing the floor.

"I'm letting him believe he has, I can't tell you what a relief it is to get away from them both for a while. They stifle me; I can never be my own man around them."

Feeling uncomfortable at Joe's outburst, I glanced at my watch. "God, look at the time, sorry Joe but we really must go, I have to be up early tomorrow morning," I exclaimed, instantly leaping to my feet.

Ceasing his pacing, Joe focused his gaze briefly in my direction, before turning his eyes towards Teddy. "Oh, so soon? Look, I'll call you later Teddy and arrange something for tomorrow."

"Yes, I'll look forward to hearing from you Joe, thanks for the meal."

Walking from the hotel room, along the patterned carpeted passageway, I caught sight of our waiter emerging from the staff lift and quickly ran over towards him.

"Thank you for tonight, would you tell the chef it was the best meal I have ever eaten?"

The waiter smiled back uneasily. "Thank you, madam, I'll tell him."

Turning to Teddy, I kissed him playfully. "Manners, my dear brother, cost nothing – always remember that."

Over the following days, Joe certainly appeared keen to experience all the high spots and places of historical interest in and around London, taking countless photos as he went. I was beginning to feel a bit of a gooseberry, knowing how Teddy felt about him, so when he eventually suggested another meal at his hotel, I made my excuses and declined the invitation.

Watching Teddy preening himself in the bathroom mirror for his big night out, I really hoped he was not going to get hurt. I had observed Joe closely over the past days and had an increasingly uneasy feeling about him. True, I found him very attractive; I could definitely understand why Teddy had fallen for him. However, both his manner and his outburst on his first night had shocked me; he was coming across as a disturbed individual. Had Steve been right to keep his distance?

***

Trembling with anticipation, Teddy waited for several minutes in the hotel's corridor before Joe finally opened the door, completely naked apart from a black towel wrapped loosely around his waist.

"Sorry, I was in the shower, didn't hear you knocking. Come on in, won't be a second, just give me time to throw something on. Mary not with you?" he asked, looking disappointed.

"No, something came up, she sends her

apologies."

"That's a shame, she's a special young lady, your sister." He looked thoughtful for a moment before continuing. "Please, help yourself to a drink from the bar, you know where it is."

"Sorry I'm a bit early," Teddy stuttered, trying hard to contain his excitement of seeing his friend's well-developed physique. "Can I pour you out something?"

"No thanks, I've just opened a beer."

Gripping a large drink in his hand, Teddy reclined briefly on one of the settees. Glancing around him at the elegant decor, he trusted that someday he would get a chance to design a room like this himself. He was thoroughly enjoying college and had already made several contacts, which he hoped would help him in his quest for employment when the course finally finished, but for the time being he could only dream.

Moments later, Joe re-emerged from the bedroom. "My pa told me I'd have to ditch the denim while I was in Europe; I feel a bit uncomfortable in these trousers, but needs must I guess." Dressed in a pair of brown flares and a crisp white open shirt, he glanced at his reflection in a long ornate mirror before continuing. "Right, I'm ready. I hope you're hungry?"

"Starving, I haven't had anything to eat all day."

Actually, Teddy had been too excited to eat, being so full of optimism of getting a chance to show Joe how much he loved him at last. It was not easy owning up to having these feelings for other men, knowing most of the population deemed such a union unnatural; in fact, up until recently, he would have been thrown in jail or been subjected to the barbaric practice of chemical castration, for even admitting to being a homosexual. He had had crushes in the past, however, he had never done anything about them, fearing rejection and humiliation. This evening was, he hoped, the pinnacle of the fantasy, which had been his dream for so long; he could not wait to feel the kiss of his lips and the closeness. How he yearned for the closeness.

They took their coffees into the lounge area of the hotel following their dinner.

"I hope you and Mary are free tomorrow night, only I've managed to get tickets for the musical 'Hair' up in the West End," Joe revealed, triumphantly removing three tickets from his wallet. "Apparently it's really a terrific production and, as it's my last evening here, I thought it a great way to end my visit. What do you say?"

"Great. I can't speak for Mary but I'd love to go, thanks."

"Do you have time for a brandy up in my room?"

"Yes, of course," Teddy responded eagerly. What he wanted to add, but was too afraid to say, was he had all the time in the world.

***

Teddy's heart rate rose as he watched Joe slowly pouring brandy into two crystal snifters. Handing one to Teddy, he sat down next to him before raising his glass.

"Cheers, thanks for making this a great start to my European adventure."

"Cheers," Teddy repeated, before taking a lingering sip from the dark liquid. It was now or never. Putting his glass down carefully on the coffee table, he sidled closer to Joe, leaning forward, his mouth parted with the expectation of experiencing his lips for the first time.

"What the fuck do you think you're doing?" Joe yelled, recoiling before leaping to his feet. "Were you going to kiss me?"

Devastated by his reaction, Teddy fled for the door.

"Wait, Teddy! Look, I'm sorry if I gave you the wrong impression, but Christ man, I'm not fucking gay."

"It's my fault; I misread the signs. I've never felt like this before you see."

"Come and sit back down, let's talk about it, I don't want you to leave hating me," Joe encouraged.

"I don't hate you, I could never hate you, but I must go. I'm so sorry ..." and with that, Teddy let himself out.

How long he walked the dimly-lit streets he was unsure of, what he was sure of was his life was a mess. How could he have been so stupid? How did he manage to get it oh so wrong?

Soon, whether consciously or unconsciously, he found himself on a park bench close to the pond where, as a child, he had passed many a happy hour with his mother and sister, feeding the swans and sailing the little boats he had meticulously created out of craft kits. Yes, life had been so much simpler then.

However, as night fell, the normally tranquil park became a notorious meeting place for all the seedy individuals looking for a cheap thrill. Sitting quietly with his thoughts, Teddy was gradually aware of someone lurking amongst the trees and shrubs behind him. Stepping out into the moonlight, the stranger coughed, turned, and began walking towards a block of toilets. Teddy rose apprehensively from his seat and followed him.

CHAPTER 4 – AN UNEXPECTED TURN

Fortunately, no one in the household was aware of the time Teddy got home the next morning. Of course, he would have been bombarded with questions if they had, and he certainly was not going to give an account of his evening experiences with anyone, let alone his family. Carefully closing his bedroom door behind him, he lowered himself wearily onto his bed before pulling the covers tightly up to his chin. Shutting his eyes, the short sleep that ensued was not a peaceful one.

Several hours later, I began banging on his door, waking him from his traumatic slumber.

"Teddy, Teddy, Joe's on the phone for you," I bellowed. For some reason, he was ignoring my cries, however I was unrelenting. "Teddy, Joe's on the phone, he's asking me whether I would like to go to the theatre tonight with the two of you."

Teddy finally responded with little emotion in his voice. "Tell him I'll call him later."

"Are you sure you don't want to talk to him now? He said he'd pick us up at six," I continued excitedly, before pushing the door open.

"No, Mary, tell him I'll call him later. Please, I'm tired, I just want to sleep."

Rounding his bed, I looked anxiously at my brother, "My god! How did you get that mark on your face? Did Joe do that to you?"

"No, Mary. Please just leave me to sleep."

"Ok, I'm going to work, but when I get back we'll have a chat? Yes?"

"Fine. Close the door behind you."

For that entire day, my mind was definitely not on the constant stream of customers I was serving in the bakery. No, it was focused entirely on my brother, as I speculated how he had managed to get such a bruise on his face. Would I ever get the whole truth out of him? Perhaps he and Joe had been in a fight; if that was the case, why had Joe sounded so upbeat on the phone?

I managed to leave work early, so I would have enough time to wash and change for our evening out. Unfortunately, there was no sign of Teddy when I arrived home, just a note to say he had gone to Steve's, would not be back in time to go to the theatre, and would I apologise to Joe for him.

***

Joe turned up at exactly six o'clock. Hearing the smooth purr of the car engine, I peeked out from behind my bedroom curtain just as the limousine came to a halt in front of our house. To be truthful, I was beginning to wish I had phoned Joe to cancel this evening, because whatever had happened between the two men must have been upsetting enough for Teddy to miss his last chance to spend time with his friend. Was I being disloyal in going out with him? Well, Teddy had not asked me not to go. Being alone with Joe would mean I could at least question him about the bruise on Teddy's face.

Outside, Joe was already out of the car and had reached the front door. "It's nice to see you again,

Joe," Mum beamed. "So, you're off tomorrow then. I hope you've enjoyed your short stay here in England?"

"Yes, it's been enlightening, Mrs Macey. Are Teddy and Mary ready?"

"Mary is, but Teddy ... Teddy's not here, I'm afraid," she replied, looking awkward at the absence of her son. "In fact, I haven't seen him all day, which is unlike him. As far as I know he's with his friend Steve. Don't stand on the door step getting cold, come on in, I'm sure Mary won't keep you waiting much longer."

Of course, it didn't take a genius, Joe deliberated, to know why Teddy was avoiding him – but if that's how he wanted to play it, by keeping his distance, then so be it. Now, slightly irritated at having to wait, he looked at his watch before starting to pace the hall. It was at this point that I appeared at the top of the stairs and began my graceful descent in a sleeveless little black dress purchased in my lunch break especially for the occasion – with Violet's help of course.

"Wow Mary, you look great."

"Thank you. You've scrubbed up well yourself."

Turning to Mum, he asked, "If it's alright with you, Mrs Macey, I had planned to go for a meal after the show, which means I should have Mary back about midnight, traffic allowing of course."

"That's fine, Joe. At least I know she's in safe hands. Have fun, both of you, and Joe – in case I don't get another chance – all the best for the coming year."

***

The route to the Shaftsbury theatre in London was

jam-packed with people. Many were already making their weary way home, but others, like Joe and me, had only recently arrived and were dressed for a night out. Entering Shaftsbury Avenue, our excitement was mounting as we finally reached the ancient doors of the theatre. Settling down in our box, we smiled nervously at each other. Then, with growing anticipation, the lights began to dim, the heavy velvet curtains slowly parted with a low clatter and the musical began – of course, we were well aware of the empty seat alongside us and I, for one, mourned the absence of Teddy.

Hours later, the exhilarating performance from the cast of 'Hair' reached the finale. As the clapping finally died down, following several curtain calls, we ultimately exited the building alongside everyone else, before bracing ourselves against the chilled night air.

"Mary, do you mind if I hold your hand? Only, I promised your mom I would keep you safe." Taken aback slightly, I tentatively slipped my hand in his and together we began to walk briskly towards the restaurant.

***

"Order anything you like," he insisted, glancing through the menu.

"I think I'll have steak and all the trimmings," I replied, believing that was my safest option from the list of gourmet delights.

"Yes, I think steak sounds good to me, too. Well, Mary, what did you think of the show? I must admit I found it thought-provoking – not only about war and love, but also about my clothes," he quipped, glancing down at his beige suit and shirt.

I grinned. "I can't see you in beads and psychedelic colours somehow; however, the whole production did totally blow me away. How they had the nerve to ... I mean, I had heard there would be a nude scene ... but ..."

"Yes, I must admit I found that part a bit uncomfortable, still, I'm glad you enjoyed it. I'm sorry that Teddy missed it though."

I looked about me uncomfortably. "Joe ... Teddy was in a bit of a state this morning. Do you have any idea why?"

Anxious about where this conversation was leading, Joe began moving uneasily in his chair. "Before I say anything I must ask: how much do you know about your brother's ... let's say, leanings?"

I looked about me awkwardly. "Do you mean, do I know he's gay?" Joe nodded. "The answer to that is yes, although he only opened up to me last week. It took a lot of courage on his part."

"Of course it did, and that's why I feel so bad about what happened last night. You see, for some reason he thought I was gay and tried to kiss me but, Mary, I can assure you I'm not."

Ashamedly, I have to admit I was actually relieved to hear this statement from this gorgeous man sitting opposite me.

"Right. So, you didn't have a fight or a struggle?"

"Why? What are you saying? No, of course not, he's my friend. Yes, I was stunned by his assumption but, no, there was no fight. When I rebuked him, he couldn't get out of the room quick enough."

"So, the bruise on his face – you've no idea how he got that?"

Joe was visibly shocked.

"Bruise? No, Mary, believe me when I say there was definitely no altercation."

I decided for the moment not to delve any further and immediately changed the subject.

"Well, are you looking forward to going to France? That's your first port of call, isn't it?"

Joe fixed his gaze on me for a moment – I could tell he wanted to continue talking about Teddy, but I definitely did not.

"Yes, I will be in France for two months and then on to Switzerland. Mind you," he began, just as the waiter arrived with our steaks, "I anticipate my stay in Europe will be much shorter than my parents had planned for me."

"How do you mean?"

"Look, Mary, I'm not expecting you to understand because your parents are great, but the relationship I have with my mine is a difficult one. They simply don't grasp why I'm not interested in the hotel business. It's caused so many arguments. Anyway, reluctantly I agreed to do this trip on the proviso that, when it's finished, if I still don't want to take over the reins from my pa, they would accept my decision. However, I made up my mind before I came here to bloody well be as obnoxious as possible, hoping I'll get up someone's nose and be sent home early."

I sniggered.

"What's so funny?"

"It worked with me; I thought you were an arrogant bastard the first evening we had dinner together."

"Now, that's a bit strong. I might be a lot of things but, as far as I know, I'm not a bastard," he laughed.

I took a long sip from my glass of red wine, plucking up courage for my next question.

"Is there a certain someone at home waiting for your return?" I asked, blushing slightly.

"Are you asking: do I have a girlfriend?"

"If you like. Well, do you?"

"No, not at the moment. There was someone though; her name's Carol, I've known her since high school – in fact, you remind me of her." He paused for a moment, apparently taking in my features before continuing, "I mean, she's English, like you, unfortunately for me we only saw each other a couple of times, her heart it seems was elsewhere. She's actually hooked up with a friend of mine now." He looked down at the glass of wine in his hand and I could not help but notice his knuckles were turning white. "I'm waiting to see how that turns out."

We finished the evening with inane chatter, because, at last, we both felt comfortable in each other's company.

***

Just after midnight, the limousine pulled up outside my house.

"Thank you, Joe, I had a really fab time tonight."

"Yes, me too. Look I'll try and write to you while I'm away, if that's ok? Somehow I don't think Teddy will want to hear from me right now."

"I'm sure he'll get over it – just give him time –

and yes, if you want to write to me, I'd like that. Well, good night."

Alighting from the vehicle, I turned and smiled at him before commencing to walk the length of our gravelled path – in the still of the night, the sound of the gravel crunching beneath my feet seemed to resonate even louder than usual.

"Wait, let me see you to your door," he cried suddenly, leaping out after me.

We stood together for a while, huddling from the cold in the porch, obviously neither of us sure what to do or say next. In the end, it was Joe who broke the silence.

"Ok, I'll see you then, take care." He leaned forward with the sole intention of giving me a quick peck on the cheek. However, unaware of his intention, at the same time I moved my face towards him, and all at once our lips found each other and came together hard and passionately, the intensity of the moment taking us both by surprise.

"Wow, Mary, I can assure you I hadn't planned that," he exclaimed, catching his breath several minutes later.

"It was nice though, wasn't it?" I beamed. "I'll see you then, Joe."

Putting my key in the lock, I turned back to look at him, briefly, before stepping forward into the warmth of the hallway. With surprising sadness, I observed him as he walked away. It was funny, I contemplated, closing the door behind me, how in a fleeting moment your life can be turned upside down.

CHAPTER 5 – NEW HORIZONS

I was oblivious to the shrill of my six-thirty alarm call the following morning. It wasn't until a sliver of sunlight penetrated through the gap in my bedroom curtains that I realised I had overslept. Shit! Why hadn't Mum woken me? Leaping out of bed quickly, I washed and dressed before deciding to grab something for breakfast at the bakery. Had last night been a dream? Had Joe and I actually had a kiss? Yes, there was no doubt about it, for a faint aroma of his aftershave still lingered in my hair. Teddy, oh my god, what was I going to tell Teddy?

Standing nervously outside his bedroom door, I knocked softly.

"Are you up Teddy?"

"Come on in Mary, I'm just getting ready to go out."

Warily, I pushed his bedroom door.

"So I see. Well you certainly look and sound better than you did yesterday. A day with Steve must have suited you."

"Yes, sorry about that, how was Joe? Is he annoyed with me?"

"He was disappointed not to see you, but he was fine about it. Look, why don't you phone him before he leaves, you might not get another chance to talk to him for a while."

Although I was encouraging him to ring Joe, I was scared; scared his new friend would enlighten him about our kiss, the kiss that Teddy had yearned for. I felt physically sick.

"I suppose he told you what happened the other night?" he asked, as he bent over to tie up the laces on his sneakers.

"Yes he did – honestly, he's not angry. He just feels frustrated you're refusing to talk to him. By the way, you've still not told me how you got that bruise?"

"I walked into a lamp post in my haste to get away from the hotel. See, not so sinister after all, just an accident, that's all it was, an accident," he repeated, trying to reassure me. "Stop looking so worried. If it makes you happy, I'll go and ring Joe now and make my peace."

The hotel manager on the other end of the line informed him, in a rather haughty tone, that Mr Carter had already checked out. Deep down, Teddy felt some relief at this outcome for, even now, he felt mortified by the whole episode, moreover his body had not yet fully recovered from the battering it had received in the park. The doctor at the hospital where he had actually spent the day had fortunately not delved too closely into how he had received his injuries. Teddy had simply told him he had been robbed in the street and, because the lighting had been so poor, he was unable to describe the face of his attacker (which was the truth) and no, he had added, he didn't want the police involved.

***

By the following July, Teddy had completed his

college course and, to celebrate his achievement, Dad surprised us all by digging deep into his pockets and taking us all out for a meal.

Sitting amongst the fine red linen and candlelit interior of the classy restaurant, Teddy suddenly produced a small black card, edged in silver, from his inside jacket pocket.

"Look everyone, I've had business cards made."

"Oh, very nice darling," Mum enthused, examining the card carefully between her fingers. "I see you're down as Edward Macey, I must say it sounds much more grown up."

"Well, it is my name, Mum; I do want to be taken seriously."

"Have you applied for any jobs yet?" Dad asked, not being one to mince his words.

"Give him a chance George, he needs some time off before he has to worry about that," scorned Mum.

Teddy looked at them awkwardly. "Actually ... I have something to announce. I've already got a job, down in London. I start in a month." Mum's face fell and her bottom lip began to quiver.

"That's great, Teddy," I cried. "It will mean you'll have to get up early like I do, instead of lying there in your pit all morning."

"Well, that's the other thing ... Mum, Dad, I've decided it's about time I stood on my own two feet, so I'm moving into my own place."

As the words spilled from his lips, Mum dropped the spoon she was holding. The implement, already half way to her mouth, splattered its contents of her half-eaten lemon meringue pie in all directions across the table.

"Don't be silly, Teddy; of course you're not moving out, we'll buy you a car. Tell him, George, tell him we'll buy him a car so he can get to work."

Dad put his hand soothingly on her arm. "Calm yourself, Mother; you'll give yourself a heart attack. Listen to the boy, we knew this day would come, it's only natural he wants to be independent, after all, he is almost twenty-one."

Unfortunately, Mum's stress levels were not diminishing. "How the hell could you afford to live there anyway? The rents are astronomical," she cried, trying in vain to clear up the mess she had created, while at the same time dabbing at the teardrops falling from her eyes.

"A couple of friends of mine, who were also on the course, have managed to get employment up in London, so we have decided to find a flat together."

"Sounds like you've already worked everything out without a thought for me or your Dad." Feeling rejected, hostility was now building towards her only son. "So who are these so-called friends of yours, have we met them?"

"No, Mum, but you will, they are very decent people. I know you'll like them."

"Let me be the judge of that," and with those sharp words the conversation came to an abrupt end.

***

Three weeks later, Teddy moved out. Even with Mum's wailing and pleading, her son was leaving home.

"I'm going to miss you so much," I began, as I sat

on the edge of his bed. "You will ring and write, won't you?"

"Of course I will Mary, and I've had to promise Mum I'll come home every other Sunday for her roast dinner. Anyway, you can come down and see me, it'll do you good to get away from here and have some fun for a change. You never seem to have fun, Mary."

He glanced quickly around his room for the last time.

"Well, I think that's everything, I'd better go." I leaned forward and hugged him tightly, not wanting our lives to change. "Mary, I'm sorry, but I must go."

Later that same morning, I began to reflect on my brother's words. It was certainly true that my life had become predicable. My entire week seemed to be working towards Saturday night, where I usually joined Violet for a drink at the Crown, before the two of us left to go on to a disco or the pictures. However, just recently, my best friend seemed to have other things to occupy her time – namely a boy she had met at the local supermarket. I wasn't jealous of Violet, no, I was mature enough to recognise that change was a part of growing up and it was inevitable that those around me would move on to greener pastures, just as Teddy had done – but where was my life going? I was still daydreaming when Violet burst into the bakery.

"Oh Mare, you'll never guess what? I've only gone and got myself a job," she screamed, leaping up and down with excitement. The moment she had left school, Violet had enrolled on a beauty course; now after two years she was fully qualified.

"Well done, Violet. Is it in the hairdressers in

Porter Street?"

"No Mare, guess again."

"I don't know ... the one by the church?"

"No. Oh, you're so rubbish at guessing. Look I'm going to burst; I've just got to tell you. It's on a cruise ship; yes, I'm off around the world, Mare, can you believe it? And Mare, I want you to come with me, they're desperate for waitresses. Just imagine the fun we would have. Think of all those gorgeous sailors. Oh Mare, say you'll come!"

Before I could answer, Mum appeared from the back of the shop.

"Mum, do you mind if I go for my break now? Only, Violet and I need to talk."

"That's fine Mary; just make sure you're back by two."

The cafe on the corner was heaving with lunchtime customers. After a short wait, we were directed to a table in the alcove.

"Well, what do you think Mare? Are you going to come with me?"

"It's just not the right time for me, Violet. Teddy has only just left home. Mum ... well, I don't think she would cope if I left too and anyway, what about Kevin from the supermarket?"

"Oh I meant to tell you, Kevin's old news. He was an idiot; I chucked him last week. Oh Mare, just please give it some more thought over the next week. The ship sails then, I really would love you to come with me."

***

The three blasts from the ship's horn announced its departure. Standing on tiptoe, alongside Violet's parents and sisters, I could just about make out my friend waving excitedly from the deck. For a fleeting moment, I wished I were going too. The coloured brochures that Violet had bombarded me with over the last few days had certainly looked enticing enough; nevertheless, I had made up my mind to stay. I had even disregarded the look of pity that exuded from Violet's eyes, as we said our goodbyes. No, I had convinced myself, I was doing the right thing. I would leave home one day, perhaps in a year, maybe two or more, but not now. The time was simply not right.

Gracefully, the vast vessel glided out of the harbour; full of emotion, we all watched until it eventually disappeared over the horizon. I turned away slowly and joined the Bell family as they solemnly made their way back to the bus station.

Two weeks later I had an unexpected visitor. Steve, looking a little sunburnt from a recent holiday in Spain, had popped round for a chat.

"How are you, Mary? Only, not seen you out and about for a while."

"Fine. I miss Teddy though."

"Well that's actually why I'm here. I had a phone call from him this morning, asking me down to London for the weekend. He said he's been trying to get hold of you, with the same invitation."

I must admit I felt a bit irritated that Steve, not Teddy, was doing the asking.

"The phone's been out of order for a couple of days. Which weekend was he talking about?"

"This weekend, if you're free that is? I know it's a bit short notice and I'm sure you have plans already, but I've got family events coming up, so it was either this weekend or next month."

I told him I would have to check my diary and get back to him. Of course, I knew full well the last entry in my little black book had been my hairdresser's appointment that was weeks ago, so, unsurprisingly, I was in fact free.

***

The slow train to Liverpool Street was exactly on time, which was a relief because I had the distinct feeling Steve wanted to engage in inane chatter; that was the last thing I wanted to do. Climbing together into an empty carriage, he plonked himself down opposite me, a stupid grin covering his face. The encroaching sounds of the slamming of doors and the whistle from the guard finally announced our departure. Rattling along the tracks, passing fields of grazing animals enjoying the late evening sun, I closed my eyes with the sole intention of averting any form of conversation. Slowing for the next station, the door swung opened and several more passengers got into our carriage, whereupon Steve decided to move from his seat to sit alongside me, nudging my arm as he did so.

"I hope you're not going to give me the silent treatment all weekend, Mary?" he probed, looking at me, waiting for a reply – there was none. "Look, you've nothing to fear from me and anyway, I've got a girlfriend at the moment."

Yes, I was well aware of that fact. Someone called Tiffany, who worked in Dorothy Perkins. Why, I thought, would he think I was interested in whether or not he had a girlfriend? It was true, he was very good-looking in a rugged sort of way and of course, in the past, I was conscious that Violet fancied him, but Violet was no longer around. So, was I in any way, shape or form drawn to this man – with deep brown eyes and long, wavy hair that just brushed the top of his collar – who was now shuffled up tightly against me? Did the fact that he was in a relationship, and therefore unavailable, make him more attractive? Obviously, he was no longer interested in me – that went without saying; nevertheless, I think the sad answer to the former question is, yes. In fact, I think if I were completely honest with myself, I had always fancied him. Oh god.

"I've just got a bit of a headache, sorry. Trains make me feel a bit nauseous, with the swaying and the fumes. Anyway, can't wait to see Teddy, or Edward, as he wants to be called now."

"Yes, what's that crap all about?"

"He thinks Teddy is too childlike, not good for his image, so it's Edward from now on."

***

Edward was standing at the entrance to the tube station, dressed, as only he could dress, in a bright green suit, topped with a pink cravat tied flamboyantly around his neck. He embraced us both before we set off in the direction of his flat.

The flat, in all honesty, was a bit poky and

completely cluttered, not surprisingly, with arty things. There was a lounge/diner at the front, which afforded a rather nice bay window, and a narrow hallway with four doors leading into a very small kitchen at the back. Opening the first of the four doors, Edward ushered us in.

"Welcome to my own personal space. It's a bit compact, I'm afraid, but it's all I really need. I thought you could bunk in with me Steve, and Mary, you can have the room next door. Donna is away this weekend visiting her family, so she said you could use it." Edward's flatmates had turned out to be two girls, Donna and Miranda, neither of whom I had had the privilege of meeting as yet.

The weekend was a whirlwind of shopping, restaurants and clubs and, before we knew it, Steve and I were back on the train home. This time, we sat next to each other from the off, mainly because the carriage was jam-packed with passengers, giving us no choice. But being so close to Steve now, did not make me feel uncomfortable any more. He had been good company over the weekend, full of fun and openly caring towards Edward, as always. Why had I not allowed our relationship to develop all those years ago? Was it too late? Had that romantic boat sailed?

Tiffany, in her ridiculously high-heeled boots and short plaid skirt which, when a breeze blew along the platform, showed an embarrassing amount of underwear, was waiting at the station when we arrived home and immediately flung her arms around him. I felt a pang of jealousy running through me, just as Steve remembered I was standing there and turned in my direction.

"See you around then, Mary, it was a great weekend. We must do it again." With that, he kissed me softly on my cheek before walking away with his arm firmly around his new love.

Arriving home twenty minutes later, I found a letter waiting for me from Joe. Lying on my bed, I carefully slit open the envelope. We had been writing to each other regularly since he had left, never anything mushy or deeply personal, just factual, about what we were doing in our daily lives – surprisingly neither of us had ever mentioned the kiss we shared on our last evening together.

Dear Mary,

Hope you and your family are well. So, my time in Europe is almost up, I can't believe I've enjoyed it as much as I have, certainly much more than I had anticipated. I've managed to take some brilliant photos, can't wait to show you. Anyway, on my way back from Germany, I've planned a stopover in London, so I hope we will be able to catch up then. As you know, I've been writing to Teddy recently, having finally made up with him, in fact I recommended him for the job he has now, so feel happy about that.

See you in less than two weeks, hopefully.

Fondly, Joe

I folded the letter and put it back in the envelope. There were four men in my life. Dad and Edward, who would always be there for me, no matter what I did. Steve, who unbeknown to him had become the lover in my dreams and, last but not least, Joe. But who exactly was Joe: my friend or potential lover?

CHAPTER 6 – AN UNEXPECTED DEVELOPMENT

Meeting up with Joe again after such a long time was quite an event for all three of us, but of course, for totally different reasons. On this occasion though, he had booked into a suite of rooms down in London, so both Edward and I had arranged to meet him at his hotel. I arrived well before Edward, who had apparently been delayed at work.

"Mary! Come on in, I can't tell you how wonderful it is to see you," Joe enthused.

I thought he looked a little heavier in stature than before, probably from all the rich food he had consumed over the year, his hair was longer and the tan had faded, however, he was still damn attractive nonetheless.

"Hello Joe. You certainly look well, Europe definitely seems to have agreed with you."

"Yes, I have to say I enjoyed the experience much more than I thought I would in many ways. How about you, Mary? You're still looking as adorable as ever."

He took my arm and guided me towards a rather grand chaise longue. I felt a little uncomfortable, not from sitting on the chaise longue, but the way he was looking at me.

"I've missed you Mary, I can't tell you how much. You've never ever mentioned that kiss we had on our last evening together in any of your letters. I've never forgotten it; I hope it meant as much to you as it did to me?"

"You've never mentioned it either, but yes, I have to admit it was a good memory."

He took my hand and began kissing my palms sensuously. I felt a tingling run through my thighs. He pulled me closer, his breath smelt sweet; I could feel the warmth of his hands as he cupped my face. Our lips were almost touching and then … someone knocking at the door brought our moment to an end. He looked at me with desire in his eyes, before reluctantly clambering to his feet.

"Teddy, we were wondering where you got to."

"Yes sorry, I got here as soon as I could. Looking good, Joe, Mary been keeping you amused, has she?" Joe turned and looked at me.

"You know Mary, as entertaining as ever. I've booked a table in the restaurant downstairs, if you're all ready to go."

"Do you mind if I just freshen up first?" asked Edward. "Only I've come straight from work and Joe, I like to be called Edward now, remember, I told you in my last letter."

"Yes, of course, sorry. The bathroom's the second door on the right." The minute Edward was out of sight, Joe took my hand again. "Mary, stop here with me tonight?"

"Joe, I can't, I've made arrangements to stay with Edward and anyway, I'm not that sort of girl."

He pleaded with his eyes just as Edward re-entered the room. Darling, wonderful Edward seemed oblivious to the steaming physical chemistry happening between Joe and me.

We actually had a harmonious meal and even my brother appeared to finally relax and enjoy himself. With the evening coming to an end, we bade Joe farewell. Stepping out into the corridor, I could not help myself, as Edward turned his back, I leaned forward and kissed Joe one last time. I have to admit that there was a part of me that longed to stay with him, but in all honesty I believed that the consequence of one night of passion would only bring misery to our relationship. He was off home tomorrow; I'd probably never see him again. No, I convinced myself, it was definitely best this way.

Following a couple of bus rides, Edward and I walked the short distance arm in arm along the, by now, almost empty side street. I could see that the lights were still on in his flat as we commenced climbing the steep concrete steps to the front door, which was promptly opened by a young woman with wild, dark curly hair.

"Hi, you must be Mary, come on in," she encouraged, greeting me with a hug. "I'm Donna, pleased to meet you at last."

Donna led the way into the front room, where about six or so other people were lounging around on brightly coloured beanbags whilst listening to some very hypnotic music. From the aroma in the room, I guessed the cigarettes they were smoking did not contain tobacco.

"Everyone, this is Mary."

"Mary, come and join us," they chorused.

Thankfully, Edward answered for me. "Thanks for the invite, but my little sister has to be up early tomorrow, so we'll say our good nights."

I did my royal wave to the group as Edward quickly guided me away to his room.

"You can have my bed, Mary. I've got a sleeping bag, I'll be fine on the floor."

"Edward," I began, "were they smoking weed?"

"Yes, they might have been. Don't look at me like that, Mary. Yes, I have tried it, and no, I'm not an addict. It's a different life around here, you have to go with the flow or you just don't fit in."

"I'm not judging you; just remember who you are and who you want to be."

I settled myself down in the single bed and closed my eyes to the world, however, I found it almost impossible to sleep – so many thoughts were running through my head, mainly about Joe. No, let's be honest, they were all about Joe. Should I have stayed with him tonight? Could he be the love of my life? Was he my future? Eventually, I drifted off into the land of erotic dreams.

The following morning, Edward woke me early, bringing me a cup of black tea.

"Sorry, we're out of milk apparently. Do you want some breakfast?"

"No thanks, I'll get something from the café at the station."

It was at this point, as I started rummaging through my handbag, that I realised my purse was missing.

"Can't find my purse Edward, it had my return train ticket in it."

"Ok, let's have a search around, it must be here somewhere." We looked everywhere, to no avail. "I'm sure no one in the flat would have taken it. Do you think you lost it at the hotel?"

I was certainly not going to start accusing anyone in the flat. Perhaps Edward was right; perhaps it had fallen out of my handbag when we were in Joe's hotel room. I had no choice, of course, but to go back to the hotel and check if it was there.

Arriving at his suite, an embarrassing thought crossed my mind. If it were in his room, would Joe think I had left it there on purpose in order to see him again? When the door finally opened, he stood in front of me dressed in a stripy bathrobe.

"Mary, wow, what a nice surprise, come on in, I was just eating breakfast. Would you like something?"

"No thanks. I'm sorry to bother you … only, I think I may have left my purse here last night."

"It's no bother Mary, in fact, I was praying you'd come back," he replied, a curious look appearing in his eye. "Any idea where you might have left it?"

To this day, I don't really know exactly how it happened. One minute we were searching for my purse and the next, we were in each other's arms, once again our lips locked in a passionate embrace, though this time his hands began searching my body. I could feel the excitement mounting in him. Here I was, alone with a man, who was unlikely to be more than fleetingly in my life, in a position that could potentially lead to us having sex. Should I put a stop to what was happening? I was still a virgin; did I want to lose my virginity to Joe, no matter how attracted I was to him?

"Wait, Joe," I cried, pushing him away. "I'm not sure I'm ready for this."

"Oh Mary, you're such a tease, you can't tell me you didn't feel the electricity between us last night, and I know you've not forgotten that last evening we had together. Come on, relax, I've been dreaming about this moment for a year and I think you have, too." He began to kiss me again; his hands were under my jumper, caressing my breasts. "You smell so nice. I want you, like I've never wanted anyone else before. I love you; there, I've said it. I think I've loved you from the first time I saw you, I want us to be together forever."

"What are you saying?" I cried, drawing back from him.

"I'm saying, I want to marry you, if you'll have me?"

"How can you ask me to marry you, Joe? We hardly know each other."

My grandparents suddenly came to mind, as I remembered my grandad's story of how he fell in love with my grandmother the minute he met her. They were married within a month and lived happily together for over fifty years. It was the perfect scenario for my grandparents, why, I was beginning to believe, should it not be the same for Joe and me?

I'm not sure whether I was just caught up with the happy memories of my grandparent's romance, but, before I could stop the words from leaving my mouth, I heard myself saying, "Yes, ok … yes, I'll marry you."

Obviously elated by my response, he lifted me up in his strong arms and carried me into the next room, where he laid me down on the bed and pulled up my skirt, before systematically removing my clothes slowly, piece by piece. I did not put up any resistance. Nevertheless, now feeling totally self-conscious by his searching eyes, which seemed to be examining every part of my naked form, I tried to slip between the sheets, but he just threw them off again, while his hands began touching and stroking my inner-most parts. His penetrating fingers were unlocking sensations I had never felt before. My whole body seemed to ache with desire. Was this true love or simply lust? My mum's words to me that good girls waited until the wedding night before giving into their man, came back to haunt me. It was too late now. At least, I thought, we are going to get married, so that makes it all right, doesn't it?

In silence, Joe lowered his body down onto mine whilst holding my wrists firmly above my head – I now found myself unable to move. This was definitely not how I had fantasied making love would be. For one thing, there was nothing romantic about it and, not only that, he seemed ignorant of the fact that he was actually hurting me. I wanted to scream out for him to stop, but my lips were unresponsive. Then, as he entered me, I felt a sharp pain and I finally let out a cry – unhappily, not one of pleasure.

The whole traumatic experience was over in a few minutes, whereupon he simply rolled off and, still without even a word or a kiss, rose from his position beside me and headed for the shower, leaving me lying alone in the crumpled sheets. What had I done?

In anguish, I lifted myself up with some difficulty and began to gather up my discarded garments. Looking around for a tissue, I opened the drawer in the table next to the bed. To my horror, I perceived, poking out from beneath a mountain of papers, my purse. I rapidly realised the only way it could have got there was if Joe had placed it there himself, because I had definitely not been anywhere near his bedroom until now. Did that mean he had planned the whole seduction by taking it out of my bag? I felt sick; violated. Dressing quickly, I was about to move towards the door when Joe re-emerged from the bathroom.

"Where are you off to? We've things to discuss. If you remember, you promised to marry me, or do you think I only asked you that to get you into bed?" My face said it all. "You do, you think I only wanted sex! My darling, I do want to marry you and as soon as I get home, I'll start making arrangements."

This was all wrong. What would Violet say? She would say marry the hunk; you'll be rich, want for nothing. However, I wanted more than just a rich husband – I wanted someone I could love and trust. Now, on reflection, I knew Joe – even after what we had just done – was not that someone. Everything was moving far too swiftly; my life seemed out of my control.

"Joe ..." I began.

"Darling, you're scaring me. Did you or did you not agree to marry me?" He stared at me, a sort of madness in his eyes. Oh god.

"Yes, I did agree to marry you."

"That's alright then," he smiled, outwardly relieved, "I think it best I go home as I had planned this afternoon and talk to my parents; after all, I've been away for a while, we have a lot of catching up to do. I'll come back in a few weeks and ask your pa for your hand, that's how you do it over here, isn't it? Oh, we'll be so happy, I know we will."

He took me in his arms and kissed me again, until, gradually, he became aware of the purse I was clutching in my left hand.

"I see you found it then."

I only managed to impart a weak smile in response, deciding not to get into a debate about exactly where I had discovered it. Of course, now he must have realised I was on to his little game, surprisingly though, the appearance of the purse didn't faze him in any way and he carried on talking about the plans for our wedding. To be frank, it was all a bit bizarre. A few hours later, Joe walked me to the Tube and we said our goodbyes, he promising faithfully to phone me as soon as he got back.

***

Eventually alighting at my station, I did not feel like going straight home; instead, I started walking towards the park to clear my head. I desperately wanted to talk to Violet, but she was on the other side of the world and, at this very minute, I wished I were too.

"Hi, you're Edward's sister, aren't you? Do you remember me? We met last year."

God, could my day get any better?

"Oh yes, Tiffany, isn't it? Steve's girlfriend, how are you?"

"I was Steve's girlfriend, he dumped me, the shit. Mind you, you look as if you've got all the worries of the world on your shoulders, hun? If you want to talk, let it all out, I'm a good listener."

Before I could stop myself, I was telling her everything, I must admit, I found it very therapeutic.

"Well, hun," she began, "I think you've got yourself into a bit of a mess. First, let me tell you honestly, everyone's first time is, well, not anywhere near as perfect as it is in books or the movies. So don't beat yourself up over it. Now, the question is, do you love him? If the answer is yes, then do you love him enough to move so far away from your family? If the answer is no to any of those questions, then write him a letter to let him down gently, before it goes any further."

Who would have thought I would have received such sensible advice from this girl, who, at our first meeting, I had considered a bimbo. She was right, of course, and the answer to both questions was no. Was it the coward's way out to write a letter? To be honest, I dreaded having to see that pleading look in his eyes again. Yes, I would sit down and compose a letter tomorrow, for the time being I just wanted a long soak in a hot bath to try and wash away the very aroma of him.

Two days later and I still had not heard anything from Joe. I had started my letter several times and the bin in my bedroom was gradually filling with scrunched up paper. It was the evening of the third day and I was sitting down with Mum and Dad for our evening meal. Dad, as usual, was listening to the news while we were eating, which always annoyed Mum, because she inevitably wanted to talk. Suddenly, the news headlines made us all stop what we were doing and listen.

"A major fire has destroyed part of the home of one of America's wealthiest families. Frank and Meme Carter, head of the Carter Hotel Group, were believed to have been in their Florida mansion at the time. Two bodies have been recovered from the blaze, but have yet to be formally identified."

We were all in shock. Mum's first thought was to phone Edward to see if he had heard anything, but what should I do? Should I try and contact the family? Theoretically, I was the fiancé of their son, but had Joe told his parents about me? Certainly I had never mentioned our unofficial engagement to anyone other than Tiffany, who now, it seemed, had taken over the role of my best friend. Stupidly, I had no phone number to call him either and anyway, why had he still not phoned me on the day he got back like he said he would? Had he had a change of heart? Had his parents forbidden him to marry me? Were my initial fears correct; did he in fact only ask me to marry him to get me into bed? However, all those questions now paled into insignificance, because the worst question of all, was one I was trying hard not to believe possible. Was Joe one of the bodies they found in the fire?

I arranged to meet Tiffany for a drink at The Crown.

"Well, I can't see that you can do very much at this stage, hun. I mean I find that after what happened in London, between the two of you – getting engaged and all that, it's a bit weird he didn't phone you like he said he would, and now this fire business. I think you have no choice but to wait for him to call you."

So that's exactly what I did.

A few days later, the news confirmed that the

remains discovered in the building were of Frank and Meme Carter. The report went on to state that their only son, Joe, who had been away at the time of the fire, had helped in identifying the bodies. Thank god Joe was alive. With everything that was happening around him, it was not surprising that I was not a priority in his life right now. He was still a friend and I felt devastated for him to have lost his parents in such a dramatic fashion.

The months went by and then, very late on Christmas Eve, the phone rang and was answered by Edward, who had come to stay over for the Christmas festivities. I could hear his voice in the hall from the lounge, although of course I could only hear his side of the conversation. Nevertheless, almost immediately, I realised he was talking to Joe.

"Hi Joe, we've been worried about you. We're so sorry about what happened to your parents. How are you keeping? Ok, wow, congratulations, yes I will, speak to you again soon," he said, before replacing the receiver.

I was beside myself with anticipation.

"That was Joe, he sounded ok. He's been busy sorting out the family business," he said, before turning to me. "You'll never guess what Mary, he's getting married and it sounded like he was actually calling in the middle of the ceremony!"

CHAPTER 7 – NEW YEAR'S CELEBRATIONS

The news of Joe's marriage obviously came as a bit of a shock, consequently I leaped to my feet and ran from the room, closely followed by Edward.

"Mary, what's the matter?"

"Nothing," I sobbed, "just leave me alone!"

"You don't have feelings for Joe, do you? Well, do you?"

Then it just poured out of me – my confession. I looked at Edward, waiting for a negative response.

"Do you hate me? I know you loved him once. Edward, do you hate me?"

"Hate you? I could never hate you. Sounds like the bastard took advantage of you. If anything, I hate him. Why did you never tell me?"

"I was ashamed of what I did, by sleeping with him I mean. I'm not that kind of girl Edward, honestly I'm not. I thought, in a mad moment, I wanted to marry him but he made a complete fool of me, I realise that now."

"Come on Mary, get your coat, we're going for a drink before Mum and Dad start asking questions. I think we both could do with one."

The Crown was heaving with Christmas revellers who had apparently all managed to escape from the last-minute preparations. Sitting in the corner, a large pint rising to his eager lips, was Steve, who immediately beckoned for us to join him.

"On your own, Steve?" asked Edward, glancing around.

"Yes, believe me, I'm quite happy about that. Anyway, it's great to see the two of you. How's life down in London, Edward?"

"Really good, got a week off so home for Mum's cooking."

"And you, Mary," he began, looking directly at me, "are you ok?"

"Fine, thanks. Bumped into Tiffany recently, you remember Tiffany, the girl you dumped."

"Oh yes, Tiffany, with those long legs and perfect …"

"I could do without a description, thank you," I interrupted. "How about that drink then Edward? Mine's a gin and tonic."

Several gin and tonics later, we were all full of the Christmas spirit and, with the jukebox blaring out the Christmas number one, Steve stood and asked me to dance. It turned out to be a great evening and, just as Violet's father called time, Steve leaned in towards me and whispered.

"What are you doing New Year's Eve, only there's the usual party here, fancy coming with me?"

I did not have to think about my answer for too long. Edward was going back up to London in a few days and I didn't fancy staying in alone on New Year's Eve, with only the television for company.

"Ok thanks, I'd like that."

***

I dreaded telling Tiffany that I had a date with her ex-boyfriend. Surprisingly though, she was fine about it, mainly because she had a new beau herself, a young doctor from the hospital whom she had met when she had taken her mother in for an x-ray. So all was well.

Of course, I was still having nightmares about Joe, questioning how he had married so quickly after proposing to me. But who did he marry? In his conversation on the phone with Edward, he had not divulged very many details, and to my brother it had sounded like he was actually calling on the day of his wedding, which I thought was an extremely odd thing to do. I still could not get over the fact that he did not ask to talk to me so he could apologise about the way he had treated me. It was as if the whole incident of our last day together had never happened. I really wished I had never met Joe Carter.

New Year's Eve arrived with all the excitement that normally accompanied the most eagerly awaited evening of the year. Mum and Dad were going out with some old friends for a meal, so everyone in our household was in a party mood. I had splashed out on a very sexy little dress, although on reflection I was beginning to feel a little reluctant about wearing it; however, after opening a bottle of wine in my bedroom and downing a couple of glasses, I was starting to feel a little bit more confident.

Steve picked me up a little late in his newly acquired car. "Sorry," he began, "I noticed I had a puncture before I left home. Got covered in grease so had to change." Then he looked at me properly. "Wow Mary, you look stunning."

"Thank you, kind sir. Well, if you think your car will get us there ok, we'd better go."

The Crown was packed to the rafters. Of course, we knew most of the people there, many of whom were more than a little surprised to see Steve and me together. We danced all evening and then the clock began the count down to 1973. On the last stroke of midnight, Steve took me in his arms and kissed me properly for the first time. I felt I was floating on air it was so magical. The kiss went on for several minutes; we were oblivious to anyone else in the room.

"Let's go outside Mary, away from all these prying eyes." He took my hand and led me through the pub doors. "Here, you'll catch your death," he pointed out, thoughtfully removing his jacket and placing it carefully around my shoulders. "Mary, you know I've never really wanted anyone else all these years. Yes, I've had girlfriends, but … Mary, I know I'm sounding corny, but I'm going to ask you anyway, will you be my girlfriend?"

That was exactly the moment Steve and I became an item.

Of course everyone was more than happy about our relationship, especially Edward. Several weeks later, I met up with him in town.

"I knew it, I knew you would end up with Steve. If only …"

"Don't say it," I said.

"Don't say what?"

"I know what you were going to say: if only you hadn't brought Joe into our lives. Well, you did and I can't do anything about that now. I'm with Steve, but please, Edward, I'm begging you, never tell him about me and Joe."

"Of course, I'd never tell anyone, especially Steve. If you remember, he didn't like him in the first place, I think he would probably want to kill him if he knew."

Those first few months with Steve, were, if I were honest, a little strange. I mean, we had known each other for years and here we were kissing at any opportunity: in Mum and Dad's front room when they were out, or in the dark in the back row of the cinema. Of course, then there was Steve's car. Now, those moments afford a little more than just kissing, nevertheless, I was very reluctant to do any more than that. I could see it in his eyes, the hurt when I refused his advances, but I was damaged goods, both mentally and physically. I knew that giving in to his animal desires would not necessarily mean our relationship was on solid ground, in fact, I believed if I allowed him to go any further, he would just use me like Joe had done and then dump me.

On one particular evening in March, we were on our way back from an evening out with friends when Steve pulled his car into a layby and turned off the engine.

"Mary, I want you to tell me honestly, do you fancy me?" I giggled nervously. "No really, I know we kiss and cuddle but when I try to touch you ... Mary, it's as if you find me repulsive."

I looked deep into the eyes of this sweet man who had been so patient with me. I realised if our relationship was going to continue, I at least owed him an explanation.

"Steve ..." I began, "someone I thought cared for

me destroyed my trust by taking advantage of me."

He looked at me uneasily. "I see. Are you going to tell me who he was? Do I know him?"

"No, no one you know," I lied, "but I'm finding it difficult to believe in anyone at the moment."

"Mary, I'm not just anyone. I've loved you for so long, it upsets me when you push me away."

I stared at him. Obviously it was not the first time I had heard the word love erupt from male lips and, not surprisingly, the declaration troubled me.

"If you love me as you say you do Steve, then you'll have to be patient or there's no future for us."

He put the key back in the ignition and restarted the engine.

"I will prove that I love you, Mary. If I have to wait an eternity, then so be it."

CHAPTER 8 – A SAD TURN OF EVENTS

The long, hot summer came to a dramatic end with thunderstorms and torrential rain, which played havoc with my asthma; consequently, I was continually popping my little pink pills. Steve and I were seeing each other most days now and, if he could get off on time from his engineering job, he would meet me straight from work, when we would grab a coffee or simply take a stroll in the park. I loved these moments together and I very soon realised I had fallen in love with him.

One day in August, I was working with Mum as usual in the shop when she revealed she was going home early because she wasn't feeling well and left me to lock up. I had been expecting Steve to meet me, however there was no sign of him by six o'clock so I pulled the door shut behind me and ran to catch the bus – missing him, as it happens, by minutes.

I arrived home some time later to an empty house. I knew Dad was down the pub as usual, but where was Mum? I called her name but received no reply. Stepping outside into her beloved garden, I continued to call, still no answer – the only sound was the squawking of the chickens and ducks that were milling around me, eager for grain. Then I saw her, my wonderful mum, lying face down in the pond.

Running towards her, I began screaming hysterically. Miraculously, from out of nowhere, Steve appeared at my side. Quickly taking charge of the situation, he lifted her limp body out of the water and laid her gently on her side upon the grass.

"Mary, quickly, go and call an ambulance." I stared blankly at him in shock and total despair. "Mary," he repeated calmly, "your mum needs an ambulance, go call one."

The ambulance arrived within minutes, sadly it was too late – Mum was already dead. In that brief moment, our lives had changed forever. The doctor said a massive heart attack had caused her to fall and hit her head, knocking her out; she drowned in the shallow water – it would have been very quick, he assured us. Nevertheless, Dad was inconsolable, blaming himself for not being there to save her.

Her funeral, ten days later, was a very sombre affair. Our local church was full of mourners, many of whom were customers wanting to pay their respects. Relatives were arriving from all over, some I had not seen for years. My Aunt Alice, Dad's spinster, older sister, arrived first and soon took charge – Dad being too traumatised to think clearly. In fact, none of us could think straight, it had been such a huge shock. Aunt Alice was a very prim and pasty-faced woman with narrowed cold eyes. She wore her grey streaked hair pulled back in a tight bun, which gave her a scary, severe expression that always frightened me as a child. In all the years, I don't remember ever hearing her laugh. Mum always said she was a bitter woman because her fiancé had jilted her at the altar, which is actually quite sad when you think about it.

Mum was only forty-eight years old; far too young to die, the vicar pointed out from his raised position in the pulpit. As the congregation sang her favourite hymns, Dad, Edward and I hugged each other, sobbing quietly for the woman who had been the centre of all our lives.

After the service, we went back at our house, where Aunt Alice had organised a buffet and drinks for the mourners. Managing to corner me in the kitchen, she announced, "I've spoken to your father and he agrees, I'm moving in. I will rent out my little cottage and come and live here to help run the household."

I was taken aback. I clearly remember Mum telling me that Aunt Alice ruled over Dad with a rod of iron when he was a boy, so I was more than a little surprised he had agreed to this scenario.

"Oh, Aunty, you don't have to do that, Dad and I can manage both the house and the shop."

"I won't be working in the shop, you can forget that," she said, turning away from me. Picking up a stack of dirty plates, she almost threw them in the sink. "Look what it did to your poor mother, working all hours and then having to look after this place, no wonder she dropped dead."

I wanted to shout at her that Mum loved this house and the shop and we didn't need her help, so go away you evil bitch – but of course, I did not. Thankfully, Steve stepped into the kitchen just at that very moment and intuitively he could tell I was upset.

"Hey you, do you fancy getting out of here for a while?"

"Yes, I could do with some fresh air, I'll get my coat." I was relieved at the chance to get far away from this witch, who seemed to think she could just step into the shoes of my beloved mum.

We drove for miles out into the countryside through picturesque villages, on and on, crossing out of one county and entering another, until we reached the top of the Downs where Steve stopped the car by a well-known beauty spot.

"I used to love coming here on a Sunday as a kid," he remarked, looking around him. "We'd have a picnic and Dad would play cricket with me, I think it was the only time he actually played with me – he was normally too busy with work."

"What was it like being an only child?"

"Lonely, most of the time. When I get married, I'm planning on a big family; at least three children, two boys and a girl."

"I see … sounds like you've got your life sorted. Well, now we're here Steve, do you fancy a walk?"

Hand in hand, we ambled down a well-kept footpath, which led us into a small copse. The overhead branches of the trees obscured the dwindling sunlight from the canopy of fallen leaves and branches, concealing the floor beneath our feet. Walking on further, we eventually re-emerged from the dim light into a large meadow full of wild flowers of every hue that stretched out far into the horizon. I took a huge breath.

"What a wonderful view into the valley from here, it's almost as if we're the only people left in the world." I sat myself down on a large boulder and Steve sat beside me. "Steve, I don't want to go home, let's find a bed and breakfast, I want to stay with you tonight."

Obviously shocked by my declaration, Steve put his arm around me. "Dear, lovely Mary, you know

I've longed for you to say you want to be with me, but it wouldn't be right, my darling. You've just lost your mum, you're upset; I'd be a total shit to take advantage of you right now."

"You wouldn't be taking advantage of me Steve; I want to sleep with you. I've felt like this for a while." He pulled me to a stand and kissed me.

"I'm taking you home Mary, if you feel the same say in a month or two, we'll arrange a weekend away, how does that sound?"

Slowly, in silence, we walked together back to the car, with our own private thoughts milling through our heads.

***

Aunt Alice proved more of a tyrant that I could ever possibly have imagined, for our home was now run like a military campaign. Meals were at set times, apart from breakfast of course, because even my aunt refused to rise before five, the time Dad was always already hard at work baking bread – except for Sundays. She also insisted he came straight home after work – no more pints and darts down the pub with the boys. Even the chickens and ducks seemed quieter and were becoming more and more reluctant to lay their eggs. Sadly, Dad refused to stand up to her, he simply sat and listened to her moaning on about how little I helped out, and how she needed more housekeeping money. Why did he allow her to control him like this? Was he scared of her? I have to admit I was a little.

Six weeks after Mum's death, I cut out a voucher

in the national newspaper for a weekend caravan holiday in Southend and sent it off. A few days later, I phoned Edward from the phone box on the corner of our road, from where I now made all my personal calls, because Aunt Alice was always lurking about when I used the one in the house, listening to my conversations and tutting about the cost.

"Hi Edward, wondered if you fancied a weekend away in a caravan with me and Steve?"

"I wouldn't want to play gooseberry Mary, you and Steve go."

"I was hoping you'd say that, but look, Aunt Alice would create merry hell if she thought I was going away for a dirty weekend, as she would probably call it, can I say I'm going down to London to stay with you?"

"My darling sister, you didn't have to ask. How is the old bat anyway?"

"Oh Edward, I'm really worried about Dad, he seems so depressed. Why don't you ask him down for the day one Sunday?"

"Good idea, I might just do that."

***

A fortnight later, Dad insisted on dropping me at the station for my supposed trip to London. Kissing him good-bye, I must admit I was feeling really guilty in lying to him. I even had to actually walk into the train station before he drove away, waving to him as I did so. I think the station master thought me quite mad as I turned around and walked out again as soon as Dad's car disappeared around the corner. I had arranged to meet Steve in Porter Street and was relieved he was already there waiting for me. It took us over three hours to drive to Southend and then another, very fraught, hour to actually find the caravan site.

The four-berth caravan was clean enough, however it was very cold and a little damp. After unpacking, Steve went out and bought some fish and chips, which always, I believe, taste far better at the seaside. Following our dinner, we took a romantic stroll along the beachfront before heading back to the caravan, where we sat huddled up together watching television on the tiny screen until I could not fight it any longer, I was tired.

"Think I'm ready for bed." I looked at Steve, who was watching a programme on golf.

"Yes ok, I'll join you in a minute," he replied, without removing his eyes from the box.

I have to say, I had expected a more enthusiastic response. I took my nightie into the minuscule shower room and changed out of my jeans and t-shirt with some difficulty in the confined space. Steve had already zipped the two sleeping bags he had brought along together and I climbed in and snuggled down nervously. Seconds later he appeared, bare- chested, in the bedroom.

"Are you sure you're ok with this, Mary? I can sleep in the other room, you know?"

"I'm sure, Steve," I cried. Pulling back the sleeping bag, my teeth started to chatter. "Quickly, it's cold in here."

Cautiously, he slipped in next to me before taking me in his arms and kissing me softly. I kissed him back. With my nightie now discarded, his caresses continued to my neck, my breasts and then the rest of my body. I felt totally aroused – my whole being was screaming out for him.

"My darling Mary, you really are beautiful," he exclaimed, drinking in the sight of my naked body. "I do love you."

"I love you too, Steve."

Carefully, he rolled on top of me, still kissing me affectionately. He was so incredibly gentle; I could not help but cry out with the sheer ecstasy of the act. As we both came to fulfilment, we held each other until we drifted off into the most peaceful sleep.

The following morning, I got up just after nine, made some breakfast and brought it back to bed.

"How about a kiss before we eat?" he smiled, pulling me towards him.

"Mr Maddox, you've an insatiable appetite, I think you want more than just a kiss."

"You may be right, Miss Macey, come here and I'll show you exactly what I want," he laughed.

I slid back into the sleeping bags and we made love again. A soggy breakfast followed some time later, then, just before midday, we took a long shower – together.

It was a wonderful weekend, one I did not want to end, but end of course it did. Late on Sunday evening, Steve drove me to the station so it looked like I'd just got off the train from London.

"I was thinking Mary, if you fancied going on holiday with me next year?"

"A holiday together? What would my aunt say? Hell, I don't care what she thinks. Yes, let's go away together. I'll have to get a passport though, I've never had the need for one before."

We kissed goodbye, reluctant to let each other go and as Steve's car eventually disappeared from sight, Dad drew up in his.

***

Months later, Aunt Alice was still living with Dad and me; to be honest, I did not know quite how much more of her controlling attitude I could take.

"Mary, did you make your bed this morning, because I noticed you didn't yesterday and for heaven's sake stop leaving your mess everywhere, I have enough to do around here looking after your father. I'm sure your poor mother wouldn't have put up with it and it would help if, from time to time, you helped with the cooking …"

It was just continuous, the nit picking, and her list of complaints towards me seemed to grow with every passing day. If it was not for Steve, I think she would have driven me insane.

Christmas came and went but, to be honest, none of us were in a celebratory mood. Mum had loved this time of the year, would do all the shopping for presents and food before collapsing in a heap saying 'never again'. Well, she would never do it again. How I missed her. Missed our little chats about womanly things. Missed her incredible cooking. But most of all, I missed the presence of her. Sometimes I would be walking along the street and for just one moment I'd think I'd seen her, perhaps someone was wearing a coat like she always wore or had their hair combed in the same style as hers. Of course, it was never my mum, my mum was dead; I would never see her again. How I missed her.

Steve took me out for dinner on New Year's Eve instead of us going to the Crown. Gazing at each over a candlelit table, he suddenly took hold of my left hand.

"Mary, I know we've only been going out a short while, but we know each other really well ..." he pointed out, as his voice began to falter. "Mary Macey, will you marry me?"

I could not believe what I was hearing. This man who I adored wanted me to be his wife. Of course, this wasn't the first proposal I had had, but this time it was for real and this time I had no doubt in my mind that I loved the man who was asking me.

"Yes Steve, I would love to marry you."

Obviously relieved by my reply, he removed a small blue box from his jacket pocket. Opening it, I screamed with joy at the diamond ring that seemed to light up the whole room. It was so perfect – so very bloody perfect. Slipping it onto my wedding finger, Steve drew me to a stand and we kissed and embraced until we were gradually aware that the entire restaurant was celebrating with us.

CHAPTER 9 – BETRAYAL

"Of course you've got to have an engagement party! If you like, I'll organise it," Tiffany enthused, taking out a pad and pen she always conveniently kept in her handbag. "Ok, you'll need a hall. How many people, do you think?"

"Hold it, Tiffany, I haven't said I wanted a party yet and anyway, Steve has some say in this decision, don't you think? It's not all about me."

Naturally, family and friends had been delighted to hear our news, although I noticed Dad seemed a bit quiet when we told him. The minute he and I were on our own together, I asked if he was ok with me marrying Steve. He looked at me, tears welling in his eyes.

"Steve is a really nice boy, I couldn't be happier for you … but your mum should have been here for this Mary, she would have loved it. She would have known all the right things to say. I don't know anything about arranging weddings. Your mum should be here," he repeated as teardrops fell freely from his eyes. I cradled him in my arms and held him close.

"Dad, I miss Mum too and yes, she would have loved to have been here to help me. You know, I'm sure she's with us in spirit. Hey," I said, trying to cheer him up, "I hope you'll make the wedding cake, three tiers at least." Dad dried his eyes and smiled.

"Leave it to me, I'll surprise you; it'll be my

masterpiece."

"Anyway, we won't be getting married until at least next year. We've got to save up first."

"Now Mary, I don't want you to worry about money, I'll pay for everything. It's what your mum would have wanted, and it's what I want too."

A week later, Steve and I were sitting in our front room, alone for once, since Dad had just taken Aunt Alice out to the shops.

"Steve, I was talking to Tiffany the other day and she thought we should have an engagement party, what do you think?"

"Yes … if you want one darling, I think it's a great idea. Changing the subject, how long do you think your dad and aunt will be at the shops?" he asked, a look of desire in his eyes.

"At least a couple of hours," I replied, "but let's not make love here, my bed will be much more comfortable, don't you think?"

***

Who would have believed how much organisation was needed for one party? I must admit, as time went on, I was more and more appreciative that Tiffany, who seemed to be in her element, had taken on the arrangements. A date was confirmed for late March and a room booked in a local hotel. To add to my joy, a letter arrived from Violet informing me she was on her way home. She had not set foot on English soil since she sailed away on the cruise ship over a year and a half ago and I had only received a couple of letters from her during all that time, probably because she was having so much fun. Anyway, I had not yet written to her about our engagement, now I knew she was coming home, I decided not to bother; I would keep it as a surprise.

On the day before the party, the phone rang and, being the only one in the house, I answered it. The line was very crackly and it took me a while to realise who the person was on the other end – when I did, I had to sit down. It was Joe.

"Mary, it that you? Oh wow. Mary, I'm so sorry." His voice kept breaking up, making it difficult to hear exactly what he was saying, but what I did understand made me recoil with disbelief. "Mary, my wife, she's left me. I made a terrible mistake, can you forgive me?" I was stunned. Who the hell did he think he was, calling me out of the blue after all this time?

"Joe, there's nothing to forgive, it was a long time ago. I've moved on and so, it appears, have you."

"Mary, I need to see you. Please, fly over here, I'll pay the airfare, first class of course. Please, I really need a friend, please come for a holiday." Was I hearing right, did this idiot think I would just drop everything and get on a plane to be with him after what he had done to me?

"Calm down, Joe. I'm sorry, as I said I've moved on …"

"At least think about it, Mary. Look, I'll give you my number. Please … just think about it."

Just to appease him, I wrote down his telephone number on a scrappy piece of paper before replacing the receiver. The call had naturally shaken me. Not because it had woken in me any desire for him – of course not, I loved Steve – nevertheless, I was scared

Joe might just be mad enough to get on a plane himself and turn up to spoil my relationship with the man I loved.

***

The morning of our party arrived. Dad gave me the day off so I could be fully involved in the last minute arrangements. I actually think he also wanted me out of the way while he finished our surprise engagement cake. Aunt Alice was flustering around in the kitchen making sandwiches as I was finishing my breakfast.

"You'd better go and have a bath while there's still hot water, Mary," she said as I sidled up to her.

"Aunty, you've never said very much about me marrying Steve. You do approve, don't you?"

"I really don't think it's my place to say." She stopped briefly before continuing. "Though, if you insist on having my opinion, there's something in the old saying, 'change the name but not the letter, change for worse, but not for better'."

I looked at her, confused.

"What it means is, your name is Macey and you're planning to marry someone called Maddox, both names have the same first letter; the saying means it's unlucky. Sorry, you did ask." Yes, and I wish now that I hadn't.

I went upstairs and ran a bath; while it was filling, I opened my wardrobe and gazed at my dress hanging expectantly on the rail. The week before, Edward had taken me shopping in Oxford Street where I had purchased this beautiful, blue, floor-length garment. Shopping with Edward had been like having Mum with me although, to be honest, he was so incredibly knowledgeable about fashion and accessories, it was almost overwhelming.

"Mary," he had begun, whilst we were taking a coffee break, "would you mind if I brought someone along to the party?"

"Do you mean Donna?"

"Donna? No, not Donna; Simon, my boyfriend."

I almost spat out my coffee.

"You really have to stop telling me these things in public places, brother dear. Simon? Where did you meet him?"

"He's a chef in a restaurant I go to, we got talking and one thing led to another. Would you mind if he came along?"

"Of course not. I don't know how Dad will react though, and then there's Aunt Alice. Hell, why am I worrying? It's my party. You're my brother and it's 1974, for God's sake. Bring him, it will be great to meet him." So, now I was not only looking forward to my best friend returning home, I was also going to meet my brother's lover.

***

Just after midday, the front doorbell rang. Violet stood in the porch way looking, quite frankly, absolutely stunning.

"Aren't you going to ask me in, Mare?"

"Violet, you look fantastic, sea air obviously agrees with you." She threw her arms around me and hugged me tightly.

"I haven't been home yet, just had to see my best

bud first. How have you been?"

"Oh there's so much to tell you Violet, drop your cases in the hall and go through to the lounge, we can talk in there." Just at that very moment, Aunt Alice came in from the garden through the French doors, carrying a small bunch of daffodils.

"Hello, and who have we here?" she enquired. Violet held out her hand.

"I'm Violet, Mare's best friend, I've been away at sea. Oh, how I love saying that."

"I see, my dear, and there's me thinking you were just a little early for the party."

"Party? What party? Mare, why are you having a party?"

"Aunt Alice, do you think you could just give us a minute? I need to talk to Violet to bring her up-to-date with everything." Tutting to herself, Aunt Alice turned and left the room.

"Who was that old bag?"

"Shhh, Violet, she'll hear you. It's my Aunt Alice, Dad's sister. I did write to you before Christmas … she lives with us now, since my mum died."

Violet looked visibly shocked. "Your mum died? Oh Mare, I didn't know, I never got that letter, in fact, I hardly got any letters from you or my family since I've been away, mainly because I've been on so many different ships. Mare, I'm so sorry. How did she die?"

We sat down and had a very emotional heart to heart – Violet was genuinely upset. Sometime later, after several cups of tea, she again broached the subject of the party.

"So you still haven't told me why you're having a

party. It's not your birthday, so what's it in aid of?"

I looked at her sheepishly. How I wish she had received my letters, because then she would know I had been dating Steve, the boy she had been obsessed with all those years ago. I started to blush.

"Come on Mare, why the hesitation?"

"It's my engagement party," I finally blurted out.

"Sorry? Your engagement party! Christ, Mare, you sly dog, I certainly wasn't expecting that. Congratulations. I've not been gone a minute and you're getting bloody married! So who's the lucky guy? I bet he's a hunk, am I right? When do I get to meet him?"

"Well, of course, you must come to the party; it's at seven, at the Hutton Hotel."

"Try keeping me away. That's a great place to hold a party, very up-market. Come on Mare, don't keep me in suspense any longer, who's the guy who's managed to steal your heart?"

"Now, don't get upset Violet, promise me you won't get upset. It's been years and you've been away." I looked at her, knowing I could not put it off any longer. "It's Steve, Steve Maddox. I'm marrying Steve."

I could see Violet take an intake of breath.

"You're marrying Steve … how wonderful. Well Mare, I must go home now and get ready for this party of yours. Seven o'clock you say? Right, I'll be there. Yes, I'll definitely be there, Mare."

She gave me a faint smile before beginning the long walk down our garden path, her overloaded suitcases causing her to stagger slightly as she did so. Of course, I realised only too well, she was far from being all right.

***

Just before six-thirty, a taxi drew up outside our house. I had spent the last two hours meticulously getting myself ready; standing now in front of my full-length mirror, I beamed at my reflection. I felt really confident in my new dress and, although my shoes were pinching my toes slightly, I didn't care. Tonight was all about Steve and me. I had decided if Violet was in a strop about our relationship, well, that was her problem; she simply had to get over it. I loved Steve and I had no doubt in my mind that he loved me. We were getting married, no question about that.

"Are you ready, Mary?" Aunt Alice called up the stairs. "The taxi's here and the meter's ticking over."

We arrived at the Hutton Hotel in good time in order to make sure our arrangements were all in place. The room looked wonderful, vases of colourful flowers were centred on every decoratively laid out table and lilac balloons had been hung around the walls. A large banner adorning the raised staging area, where the DJ was setting out his equipment, read:

'CONGRATULATIONS MARY AND STEVE ON YOUR ENGAGEMENT'.

An over-excited Tiffany was the first to greet us.

"Oh hun, do you love it? I hope you do. Steve's already propping up the bar, by the way, with a few of his mates."

"It looks great Tiffany, thank you so much for all your hard work. I don't know how I would have managed without you. Well, I'd better go and find my fiancé before he gets too worse for wear. "

There he was, looking more handsome than ever, in a dark blue flared suit. "Here's my girl," he cried, greeting me with a kiss before taking me to one side. "Mary, you look good enough to eat, can't wait to get you to myself. By the way, I've got a surprise for you. I've booked us a room tonight, here at the hotel, look I've got the key," he said, jingling it enticingly in front of me. "You don't fancy going up and having a quick look now, do you?" he asked with a twinkle in his eye.

"Steven Maddox, we have over a hundred guests arriving any minute, you'll have to wait a little longer," I lowered my voice to a whisper, "but, believe me, you'll not be disappointed." I kissed him hard and I felt him melt with the anticipation.

An hour and a half later and the party was in full swing. Even the appearance of Edward and his boyfriend Simon seemed to have gone down better than I had ever hoped. I felt really proud of Dad when he shook Simon's hand, knowing that deep down he was feeling uncomfortable with the whole situation, although I think Aunt Alice in her naivety just thought he was a good friend – I certainly was not going to put her right. I must say, seeing my brother so visibly happy gave me an immense amount of pleasure.

Violet had not yet put in an appearance; perhaps, under the circumstances, she had had second thoughts. Anyway, everyone who was there seemed to be enjoying him or herself, especially Tiffany, who had been draped over her doctor boyfriend ever since the disco had begun. Then, just before the food was wheeled out, Violet finally made an entrance in a low-cut red dress, which – quite frankly – left little to the imagination. Dragging along beside her was a leather-clad, spotty male, who I had never clapped eyes on before.

"I'm glad you could make it Violet, I was beginning to wonder where you'd got to."

"Oh Mare, I told you I wouldn't have missed this evening for the world. I hope you don't mind but I've brought Terence along. Terence, this is Mare, my best friend."

"Pleased to meet you, Terence. It's a free bar so please get yourself a drink," I said, wondering where on earth Violet had found him at the last minute; he was certainly not the type of man she was usually attracted to.

"Where's your fiancé, by the way?" she asked, glancing around, "I want to congratulate him, too."

"He's talking to the DJ. I'll tell him you're here when I get a chance."

"Not to worry, I'll go over to him now," and with that she headed off in Steve's direction before I had time to say anything more.

Terence, without having uttered a word, had already left for the bar. Not unsurprisingly though, my eyes followed Violet across the room and, as she reached Steve, I felt a pang of jealously hit the pit of my stomach as I watched her throw her uncovered arms around his neck, watched as she pressed her body hard up against his, while she kissed my fiancé full on the lips in front of my family and friends.

How bloody dare she! Within seconds, I arrived at his side.

"There you are, Mare. I was just saying to Steve

how lucky he is to have you."

"Of course you were, Violet," I replied through gritted teeth before turning to look at my fiancé. "Steve, the food's being brought out, can you ask the DJ to announce it please?"

Steve, seemingly taken aback by Violet's enthusiastic embrace, disentangled himself from her grasp and winked at me, knowing full well from the look on my face that I was furious.

"Certainly, darling," he said, before his face broke out into a grin.

Several hours later and the increasingly drunken party was coming to an end. Swaying slightly, Steve informed me he was just going up to our room to get another film for his camera. When, after about fifteen minutes, he had not returned, I decided I had better go and find him, imagining him passed out on the bathroom floor in a sea of vomit. I really hoped that was not the case, because I was so looking forward to a night of wild passion.

Reaching our hotel room, I knocked softly and called out his name. There was no reply. I tried the door – disturbingly, it was not locked. I pushed at it gently, only to find the room beyond was in darkness. Feeling for the light switch on the wall, I flicked it on. The devastating sight that met my eyes shattered my future dreams in an instant. Steve was lying in the large double bed and mounted on top of him was a writhing, naked Violet, who turned her head in my direction and smiled a victorious smile.

"Steve!" I screamed hysterically, before sprinting from the room and I kept on running right out of the hotel. Jumping into a waiting taxi, choking with emotion and with my mascara now smeared all down my face, I commanded the driver to take me home.

Home – what the hell should I do now? My whole life had been turned upside down. I tore up to my bedroom and ripped off the dress I had been so joyful to wear. Now I did not even want to look at it. How could they? My so-called best friend and the man I was going to marry – betrayed by both of them. I had to leave, of course: this house, this town, even this planet if I could. I pulled my suitcase down from the top of the wardrobe and began throwing clothes into it randomly. Dad would surely understand my going if he knew the awful truth, I know he would. I must write him a note.

Standing in the hallway, I reached for the pad next to the phone. It was then I noticed it, all crumpled up in the little green litterbin – Joe's phone number. I began to dial. His voice at the other end, for some reason, calmed me. In minutes, it was all arranged. With my newly acquired passport securely in my pocket, I said goodbye to my life and headed off towards the unknown.

PART 3

CHAPTER 10 – JOE CARTER

"I'm sorry Frank, we have to operate now or we'll lose her. She's lost a lot of blood; a hysterectomy is the only answer." The doctor's words brought shattering news on what should have been a day of celebration for the Carter family.

The year was 1950, a baby boy had been born to Diana and Frank Carter – finally, the dream had been fulfilled. A boy, whose destiny was already set in stone, at least as far as his father and Grandfather Bill were concerned. For he was the future; a future that would see the continuation of the Carter dynasty created by Bill and his late wife Martha from their small Manhattan apartment more than thirty years earlier. The story was that Bill, who had had a strong head for business from an early age, had made some good investments on the stock market well before the Wall Street crash of 1929, consequently, not only did they manage to buy their own apartment but, eventually, the entire block. By the time Frank was born, the family had already moved out of Manhattan to Miami Beach, Florida, where they purchased the first of a chain of hotels. Bill rapidly became known globally as the man with the Midas touch. These were truly the golden years.

The minute Joseph William Carter took his first breath, the nurse wrapped him tightly in a soft white blanket and handed him, as she had been ordered, to his grandfather. With his own health rapidly failing,

Bill gently kissed his grandson's forehead for the first and the last time, before handing the infant to his anxious father.

"Frank, do whatever you have to do, but make sure he knows what is expected of him. I won't be around to see it, but you make damn sure he learns what it means to be a Carter," Bill emphasised, grabbing hold of his son's arm with his last bit of strength. "Your mom and I didn't give our lives to see our company end with you."

"Pa, you know I love the company as much as you do, I promise I won't let you down."

Over the following few days, surrounded by prayer and every conceivable medical know-how, Diana lay fighting for her life. Although she was weakened by the birth, her spirit was not diminished and was still as strong as ever. Nonetheless, it was not until almost a week later that she was able to hold her baby for the very first time and, from that moment, he became the centre of her world.

She had been married to Frank for over two years. They had first met when the businessman was visiting California, looking for someone to produce a magazine to promote the Carter Hotel Group. The hazel-eyed, dark-haired beauty had already built up quite a reputation as a commercial photographer on the east coast, a somewhat unusual occupation for a woman at that time. When they were introduced at a party being held by a Hollywood socialite, Frank was immediately bowled over and commissioned her for the project. Used to getting his own way, the tall and steely blue-eyed, mogul soon swept her off her feet. Love swiftly engulfed them, leading to a lavish wedding less than a year later, attended by film stars and politicians both past and present.

The minute they purchased Fouracres, their west coast Florida mansion on the outskirts of Naples, Diana set about making changes to their vast home. First, of course, she needed somewhere to work, as she insisted on carrying on with her career even though her new husband was initially strongly against it. Still, Frank loved her so much he finally gave in to her demands and instructed the builders to turn part of the enormous basement into a studio and darkroom.

Photography was not Diana's only passion; she also adored horses and had done so since she was a small child. As a wedding present, Frank surprised her with a strikingly handsome, chestnut quarter horse and even went as far as having a barn and corral built in the immense grounds of their beachfront property. The new Mrs. Carter was now the happiest she had ever been in her life; she had an adoring husband, who she loved, an ever-expanding career, and a horse she named Cheyenne. Most evenings, she would saddle up at the coolest part of the day and ride out along the beach where the salty waves lapped gently at her mount's hooves. The excited pair would gallop along the white sands, enjoying the feeling of freedom, without a care in the world. She truly felt she was the luckiest woman alive.

Now they had their son and, as she cradled her tiny baby in her arms, she vowed to never let anyone or anything ever hurt him.

Before Joe had even taken his first step, Diana placed him on the back of his very own pony. His mother's love for horses was almost immediately ignited in him and, as he grew older, they would spend hours together riding and grooming and generally caring for their animals.

The Carter household was certainly a happy environment to grow up in, until the devastating day came when everything changed. Joe remembered clearly it was a Monday; how he hated Mondays. It started with Diana dropping him off at school because he had missed the bus – always an embarrassing scenario when you're a teenager, your mum having to drop you off at school. When he arrived back at Fouracres that same afternoon, he was surprised to see both his parents waiting for him. For a split second, he thought he was in trouble for something that had happened at school that morning, until he saw the forlorn look on their faces. They sat him down and slowly, so he could comprehend what they were saying, broke the shattering news.

Diana had been diagnosed with breast cancer. He felt numb. United in heartache, they held each other tightly, not wanting to let go. He loved his mother so much, the realisation that one day soon she would not be with him was almost too much to bear. They made a pact between the three of them that night that they must carry on as normal, so the following day and all the days that came after, that is exactly what they tried to do. Nevertheless, most of the time, Joe was simply going through the motions. For him, life could never be normal again.

Over the next few months, Diana's health declined rapidly, to such an extent that most days she was confined to a wheelchair. Eventually, she was unable to ride her beloved Cheyenne and instead she had to be content in watching Joe putting the animal through his paces; with such mature skill it brought tears to her eyes.

On one particular day, Joe was riding around the corral as usual, with his mother looking longingly on with pride. Reining to a halt in front of her, he dismounted effortlessly.

"I think we'll do well tomorrow at the rodeo, Mom, what do you think?" he said, tying Cheyenne to a wooden post rail.

"I think, dear boy, you could be right. Just make sure you give him less rein on the turns; he's been doing this a lot longer than you have," she paused, "sweetheart, do you think you could run into the house and fetch my shawl? I'm feeling a little chilled."

"Of course, Mom. Do you want to go inside?"

"No, I'm happier staying out here a bit longer." She smiled at him and he leaned down and kissed her. "Now don't go making any noise, you know your pa's working hard in his office."

Arriving at the house, Joe ran up the stairs, taking two at a time. His parents had had separate bedrooms for a quite a while now, mainly because, on bad days – and there were certainly lots of those recently – Diana needed total peace and quiet. There it was, her favourite multi-coloured shawl, draped neatly over the chair beside her bed, a memento from a photo shoot in Mexico. He lifted it up gingerly and held it to his chest. It smelt of her. He breathed in deeply, enjoying the feeling the aroma was having on his senses. Just as he was about to exit the room, he heard a noise coming from somewhere along the landing. He knew his father was working down in his study with his secretary and, as it was Cassey, the new young maid's day off, there was no reason to suppose that there was anyone else in the house.

Curiosity got the better of him as he made his way along the corridor. He stopped and listened. There it was again, the sound seemed to be coming from one of the guest bedrooms. He stood outside the door for a minute or two before trying the handle. The room beyond was empty but, as he was about to close the door again, he thought he heard a woman's laugh coming from the en-suite. Slowly, he moved towards the bathroom door. It was not closed so he pushed it slightly. In the steam-filled room, he could just about make out the naked figures of a man and a woman. The woman was bent over the bath and the man, in an excited state, was thrusting at her eagerly.

He felt sick. Fleeing from the room, he ran back down the stairs and out into the fresh air. Still clinging onto the shawl, he reached his mother's side.

"Joe, are you ok? You look quite flushed."

"I'm fine Mom, just been running, not as fit as I thought. I love you, Mom." She looked at him quizzically.

"I love you too, Joe, are you sure there's nothing wrong?"

"No Mom, there's nothing wrong." Opening the gate of the corral, he continued, "I'll just take Cheyenne through his paces one more time, we don't want to let you down tomorrow."

***

The knowledge that his own father, who he had always idolised, was making out with his twenty-something secretary, hung heavily on the young boy's shoulders. He began to distance himself from him, becoming even more attentive towards his mother, wanting to protect her from finding out the awful truth that was eating away at him daily.

Of course, now he was aware of his father's infidelity, he was continually suspicious about what was going on behind closed doors. Not feeling man enough to confront him about his behaviour, Joe's plan was to catch them 'at it' in order to instigate some kind of confrontation, which he almost managed to do on several occasions, by simply entering his father's office without knocking. Unfortunately for Joe, he was merely forced to smirk inwardly to himself, as the startled pair adjusted their attire with some lame excuse or another.

"Miss Winter dropped her files," or "Miss Winter has something in her eye," or, the best one to date, "Miss Winter thought she saw a mouse and just happened to jump in my lap," … with her skirt around her waist? Yeah, right.

On the morning of his sixteenth birthday, something snapped and he found he could not hold the secret in any longer. Frank had bought him his first car, a cherry-red Mustang convertible, the dream of most boys of his age and proudly presented it to him after breakfast.

"Well son, jump in and we'll take it for a spin," Frank encouraged, disappointed at Joe's lack of enthusiasm.

"Is this a bribe, Pa?" he asked, running his finger

along the bonnet of the shiny new vehicle, before turning and directing a glare towards Frank, "only, I'm not so easily bought."

"What the hell are you talking about, son? It's your fucking birthday present, are you saying you don't want it?"

Folding his arms, Joe leaned against the car. "I know, Pa. I know about you and that slut of a secretary."

"What do you think you know, boy?"

"I've seen you two together, on more than one occasion, I've kept quiet until now, but Mom deserves better."

"You leave your mom out of this. Do you hear me? I love her and always will, but a man has needs. I have needs, your mom would understand."

"Really? Shall we go in and ask her?"

"Like I said, boy," Frank drew up to his full height, his broad build was now towering over his son, his recently acquired gold-rimmed glasses steaming slightly, blurring his vision as his eyes narrowed, "a man has needs, you'll know what I'm talking about when you're older. If you want to be the one to break your mom's heart, bring her even more pain, go ahead."

Just at that very moment, the sound of Diana's approaching wheelchair made them both turn around.

"Joe, my darling boy, you left the table before I could give you my present." Balanced on her knees was a square shaped box, wrapped in silver paper. "Here, I've been wanting to give you this for weeks. Open it then, it won't open itself."

Tearing at the paper, Joe cried with joy. "Oh

Mom, it's great, a camera."

"I know you've already got one, but I thought you were old enough now to appreciate a really good one. It's the one I use, a Nikon F. I'll show you how to use it properly, after you and your pa have had your drive. Go on then, the two of you, at least once around the estate."

Joe kissed and hugged Diana, before reluctantly climbing into the driver's seat next to his father. The two didn't speak for the entire journey and Joe never brought the subject of his father's infidelity up again – at least, not that year.

***

Several months later and Joe was becoming quite proficient at using his new camera. Diana tried to teach him everything she knew, even down to the processing of the black and white films, using the poisonous chemicals that were always kept safely under lock and key in a metal container in the darkroom.

"I think I'd like to do this as a career, like you, Mom," he blurted out one day as he wheeled her around the grounds, taking pictures as they went.

"Don't let your pa hear you say that, you know he expects you to take over the company."

"He can expect. Seriously, Mom, I want to go to college after I finish high school and study photography."

"Joe, I'm sorry, that simply can't happen, you know full well your pa wants you to do a business course. It would break his heart, and your

Grandfather Bill would turn in his grave if you didn't keep the Carter Empire going. Promise me you'll carry out his wishes."

Joe tucked the red tartan blanket more securely around Diana's legs and, deep in thought, pushed her back to the house.

***

Winters in Florida were usually quite mild however, this particular season, they experienced a light dusting of snow. Finally, with the emergence of spring, the air began to warm to a comfortable heat and the holidaymakers started to arrive in their droves. A busy time for everyone in the holiday trade, but an especially busy time for Frank, who now not only had hotels up and down the Florida coast line, but also in California and other parts of the United States – the empire was continuingly expanding. The consequence of this was he was always in demand for meetings and jetted off wherever he was needed; in fact, it was becoming a rare occurrence to find him at home these days. Of course, Joe was more than happy having his mother to himself.

Then, one day, a day embedded forever in Joe's heart, he was alarmed to see an ambulance and the doctor's car parked in front of the house on his return from school. He tore up to his mother's bedroom and burst through the door. Two doctors and Diana's private nurse were gathered around her bed. All three turned and looked at him with despondent faces.

"Mom?" he cried, sprinting to her bedside, before crouching down next to her and taking her hand in his. "Mom, can you hear me?"

"Joe," said one of the doctors, lightly touching the boy's shoulder, "your mom is fading fast, she can hear you but she is too weak to speak. We'll leave you for a while so you can say your goodbyes."

Alone with his mother, he leaned forward and kissed her softly.

"Mom, I'll try and get hold of Pa. Mom, don't leave me. Mom, I love you. I will always love you."

Making a final effort, Diana opened her eyes and smiled faintly at her only child – sadly no sound came forth from her pale-dry lips. Then, as he held her close, her breathing became shallow and her spirit left her body and drifted into the next world. With tears burning his eyes, Joe realised his life could never be the same without her.

How long he lay by her side, he was unsure of, but eventually the nurse very gently told him she had to see to Diana's body. Closing the front door behind him, with the wailing sound of Cassey still ringing in his ears, Joe headed out to the barn. Cheyenne, ignorant of the fate of his mistress, greeted him as usual with a whinny and started pawing at the parched ground with his hoof.

"She's gone, Cheyenne, but I'm still here and I love you just as much as she did," he said, stroking the steed's soft, velvet muzzle, "we have to be strong, she would want us to be strong."

He saddled up and led the eager animal outside. Swinging himself into the saddle, Joe felt his mount tremor with anticipation as they headed straight out to the shoreline. Although the sun had long disappeared over the horizon, the glow from a full moon guided them on their way, its reflection on the vast ocean dancing tantalizingly amongst the gentle lapping waves. They galloped hard with the warm salty air in their faces; cooling air, which was refreshing Joe's lungs and at the same time drying his falling tears, as they rode on and on, until finally the beach came to an end. Reining Cheyenne to a halt, he sat in the saddle for several minutes, contemplating an existence without his mother who had meant more to him than life itself, before reluctantly turning the animal's head back towards Fouracres.

CHAPTER 11 – HIGH SCHOOL

The funeral, a few weeks later, certainly did not go unnoticed. Just like Diana and Frank's wedding, film stars and politicians – even the Vice President – attended, so important had the Carter family become. Of course, there was no problem with accommodation for all the mourners and every hotel in the near vicinity was eventually full to capacity. The morning of the funeral arrived and Frank sat impatiently waiting for Joe to join him for breakfast. When he did, Joe ignored his father and simply sat down at his usual place at the vast dining room table, while a desolate Cassey, her long dark brown hair tied back in a tight ponytail, exposing her shoulders hunched in grief, brought him his breakfast of scrambled eggs and juice.

"Cassey, are you going to be ok?" Joe asked, touching the maid's hand as she placed the plate of food before him.

"Miss Diana was so good to me. I still can't believe she's gone, Master Joseph."

"My mom thought the world of you too, Cassey," he replied, looking up into her deep chestnut eyes.

"Thank you, Master Joseph," she cried. "Thank you," she repeated, before turning and walking away with a heavy heart, leaving the two men alone in the room.

"Joe," Frank began, "I know this is hard for you – it's hard for me too – but your mom had been sick for a very long time; it was inevitable this day would come, we have to pull together to get through this."

Joe stared out in front of him.

"Joe, are you listening to me? It's just you and me now ..."

Joe's expression quickly turned to anger as he directed his face towards his father. "It will never be just you and me, or have you forgotten Miss Big Boobs already?"

Frank jumped to his feet and pushed his chair back so hard it toppled over and crashed to the wooden floor. "I won't have you speaking about Miss Winter like that; you will show some respect, my boy, or you and I will come to blows."

"Respect? You're an arsehole, Pa. Did you respect Mom when you were screwing your mistress in every part of this house? No, I will never show you respect, you don't deserve it," he roared, before fleeing from the room.

***

High School was now Joe's place of sanctuary. His friends were naturally full of sympathy following his mother's death, especially his closest friend Angel Perez. The two boys had been an unlikely pairing right from the start, mainly because they were from totally different worlds. In comparison to Joe's lavish life style, Angel's family lived in a modest house with a modest backyard. His father was an officer in the police force and his mother a kindergarten teacher. Diana had always encouraged the friendship between the two boys, believing it didn't matter about someone's background; if there was a connection, let it happen. They had been inseparable since they first met at the age of ten, doing everything together from sports to socialising. Girls had yet to come into the equation in a big way but, when they did, well it was inevitable it would test their relationship to the max.

Who first set eyes on Carol is still up for debate, but the young English girl certainly had the wow factor. It was their final year at Senior High School and, as Carol strutted past with her long legs and a smile that took your breath away, both boys' heads turned and their eyes followed her as she chatted away to her friends.

"Man, who was that chick?" Angel gasped.

Joe, still drooling, took a while to reply.

"No idea. Think I'll go and introduce myself though," and with that, he headed off in her direction. Not wanting to be left behind, Angel followed closely at his heels.

"Hi," Joe began, walking backwards, trying to get her attention, his hands deep in the pockets of his jeans, "you're new? Let me introduce myself, I'm Joe and this gawping Latino is Angel and you are?" Carol stopped her conversation and looked him up and down.

"That was rude, I was actually talking to my friends and you just interrupted a very deep conversation."

"You're not American?" Joe exclaimed, surprised.

"Give the boy ten out of ten. No, I'm not," she answered, causing the two girls beside her to giggle.

"Are you Irish? My grandfather had Irish blood. Are you Irish?" he repeated.

Carol heaved a sigh. "No, I'm not Irish. Now please get out of my way, we've a class to get to." She tried to walk on further, but Joe was not going to give in so easily.

"English then? Yes, you have a look of an English rose and your eyes are hazel, aren't they? My mom had hazel eyes."

Carol stopped and glared at him, "I refuse to be late for my first lesson. I don't want to be impolite, but please get out of my way."

"I will on one condition, if you agree to meet me in the cafeteria at lunchtime so I can buy you a burger and a coke. I want to show you some good old American hospitality."

"I'll agree if you will only get out of my way now!" With that, Joe stood aside. "It's Carol, by the way, and yes I'm English and proud of it."

"There, that wasn't so difficult, was it? See you later, Carol," said Joe, winking at her as she and her giggling friends went on their way.

"Nice one, man," said Angel, full of admiration, "do you think she'll actually turn up?"

"Yes," Joe contemplated, "I think she might."

Now, deep in thought, Joe began to imagine being parked at Glade Point with Carol cuddling tightly up beside him. There was something special about this girl that was making his heart pound faster, something special that was drawing him to her. In the meantime, he had a lesson to go to and he could not afford to be late again.

**

At exactly one o'clock, Joe managed to find an empty table in the cafeteria and immediately started scanning every girl who came into view. When he eventually spotted Carol, looking just as delectable as he remembered, he jumped to his feet and beckoned her over.

"Carol, over here, I've saved you a seat."

Weaving her way towards him, he quickly realised her friends were still in close proximity.

"I thought it would be just you and me?"

"You know what thought did. Besides, I don't know you – you could be a maniac or something; consider them my bodyguards." Carol looked around the crowded room. "Anyway, no one could possibly be alone in here."

Joe sighed. "Ok, I guess I'll have to buy you all lunch, so what would you ladies like?"

***

Half an hour later, they left behind the confines of the cafeteria and made their way out into the open air. Heading towards the recreational area, having finally lost the company of Carol's friends who apparently had a band rehearsal to get to, they reached the shade of an aged tree. Gallantly, Joe placed his jacket down on the grass for Carol to sit on.

"So, how was your first morning?" he began, leaning his back up against the trunk for support.

"Ok, a lot different from home, but ok I guess."

Joe was trying desperately to think of what to say next. What was Angel's advice? Get her to talk about herself, to show you're interested in her mind not just

107

her body.

"So, Carol, why the move to the United States?"

She lay back on his jacket, looking up into the tree. "My good old mum married a colonel in the American Air Force who decided he wanted to retire out here in Florida. I didn't want to come, but she wouldn't leave me behind; no family left you see, all gone."

"Oh, I'm sorry. What, everyone? It's just you and your mom?"

"That's what I said, didn't I?" she shouted, scrambling to her feet, "they're all bloody dead," and with that, she gathered up her books and ran back towards the school building, leaving Joe alone and slightly bewildered.

Regrettably for him, his day was not about to get any better. Arriving back at Fouracres later that afternoon, he noticed his father's car parked in the driveway. Damn, he really did not feel in the mood for a confrontation, not today.

Hearing his son enter the house, Frank immediately stepped out of his study.

"I would like to speak to you for a minute, Joe, in my office please."

Reluctantly, Joe followed him through the door and immediately he noticed the bottle of champagne and three long-stemmed glasses on his father's desk.

"Joe, I think you know Miss Winter."

"What's this all about Pa? I've got a project I need to finish."

"It'll not take long, my boy. I wanted you to be the first to know. Miss Winter, Meme, has agreed to be my wife."

Joe stood shaking his head. "Now, why does this not surprise me?"

It was at that exact moment the phone rang. Frank mumbled something about an important business call he was expecting and left the room to answer it in the hallway. Alone with Meme, Joe moved about awkwardly.

"Come here, Joe, give your new mom a kiss," Meme cried, her ample bosom straining against her tight sweater. Holding out her arms, she reached for him and, before he could move a muscle, her large red-painted lips engulfed his; he could clearly see her protruding nipples, which were now thrust firmly against his chest. Lowering her right hand, she began rubbing his genitals. "I think," she whispered softly, "you and I will be great friends."

Repulsed at the very thought, he removed her hand from his manhood. "I think not, bitch, you disgust me. My pa may be under your spell, but I never will; my standards are much higher." He managed to release himself from her grasp seconds before Frank re-entered the study.

"If that's all Pa, may I go now?"

Frank, ignorant of the altercation that had just taken place between his son and his fiancé, nodded in acceptance of his chilled reaction to the couple's news.

Opening the bottle of champagne, Frank handed Meme a glass. "He'll come round, Meme, just give him time."

Sipping slowly at the bubbling liquid, the red-head smiled inwardly to herself. "I'm sure he will Frank; he's his father's son after all."

Putting down his glass, Frank took her in his arms and began to caress her breasts. "You know, you drive me crazy, you're so fucking beautiful," he said, kissing her ardently, before reluctantly breaking away. "I must go up and talk to him, to try and make him understand," he said. "Afterwards we'll celebrate properly, just the two of us – why don't you go and run a bath with lots of bubbles."

Leaving the study, he followed Joe up to his room. Knocking before entering, he found his son sprawled out on his bed, staring into space.

"Joe, I realise this is hard for you to take. I just needed to tell you, I loved your mom with all my heart and Meme, no matter what she thinks, is not her replacement. We won't be getting married until next year at least and it will be a quiet wedding. I just wanted you to know that, that's all."

"Pa, I don't want to talk about it; it's your life, your mess." Joe closed his eyes tightly. Frank realised there was no further discussion to be had, so turned reluctantly and left.

***

Less than a year later, the last few weeks of his final year at high school stretched out in front of him. Exams had been completed and it was now time to look forward to the prom and the organisation of the yearbook. Because Joe was still heavily into photography, he volunteered to be on the yearbook committee as the official photographer. This meant he had permission to take everyone's picture – from the teams to the cheerleaders and, in fact, to every single individual in his year. He was in his element.

Of course, he was now able to take Carol's picture without any questions being asked, which he did on more than one occasion, sometimes without her realising it – it became his obsession. Developing the black and white photos in his mom's dark room, he found himself studying Carol's face more closely. She had hardly acknowledged him since their encounter on her first day, but he had not yet given up hope of securing her affection.

One Saturday morning, when Cassey had come in to clean his room, the maid happened to come across one of his many pictures of Carol.

"Master Joseph," she began, "when was this taken of Miss Diana? She looks so young."

Joe snatched it from her hand. "This is not my mom, Cassey, it's a girl called Carol from school."

"Really?" she said. "I know it's in black and white but they look so alike, they could be sisters," she pointed out.

Joe looked at the picture more closely. Why had he been so blind not to realise it before? It was so obvious now; Carol was the spitting image of his mother! Was that why he felt so attracted to her?

***

For the first weeks of his summer vacation, Joe spent the time either riding Cheyenne or hanging out with Angel. Of course, the main topic of conversation between him and his father was which college he was going to. Respecting his mother's final wishes to take a business course, naturally pleasing Frank at the same time, he applied to go to the University of Florida and was accepted once his grades were realised.

Not wanting his son to be simply hanging aimlessly around the house for the entire holiday, Frank decided to give him a job in one of his hotels. Naturally, Joe thought it would be a junior managerial position – but no such luck.

"My pa, your grandfather, made me start from the bottom and work up, so I could understand each and every job. With that in mind, my boy, your first position will be as a porter, we'll see how you get on from there."

Needless to say, Joe hated every minute. By the time his course finally began, it was actually a huge relief.

Angel, in the meantime, had secured a job in a warehouse whilst he waited for his nineteenth birthday, at which time he intended to apply to join the Florida Police Force, following in his own father's footsteps. Now, both boys had their futures mapped out in front of them.

Unfortunately for Carol, she found herself in limbo, not really knowing what she wanted to do with her life apart from shopping. To be honest, she was still pining for her home in London. She prayed that one day soon her mother would wake from the insanity that brought them here following a marriage to a man she barely knew. A man whose very presence made Carol's skin crawl, simply by the way his eyes seemed to pursue her as she walked around their house. Yes, she trusted that eventually they would return to England.

One Tuesday, while Carol was waiting for a bus,

Joe and Angel pulled up beside her to see if she wanted a lift – and she accepted readily.

"Not seen you around for a while, Carol, how are things?" Angel asked, turning in the passenger seat to gaze at the young beauty.

"Ok I guess … no, actually, I'm bored. I've been trying to get some casual work, while I decide what I want to do, but there's not much around." She opened her bag and took out a pink lipstick and started applying it heavily to her full lips. Joe looked into the rear view mirror, still overcome with the fact that the girl of his dreams was actually occupying the back seat of his car.

"I could probably get you a hotel job if you're interested?" he asked.

"What, in one of daddy's hotels?" she mocked. Joe was taken aback by the sarcastic tone of her reply.

"I'm not pushing it; would you be interested or not?"

"I guess so, what sort of job?"

"Waitressing or housemaid, something like that." Glancing in his mirror, Joe caught her rolling her eyes.

"Ok. I guess I have to begin somewhere."

A week later, Joe phoned Carol to tell her the good news. He had found her a waitressing position, starting immediately. He arranged to pick her up early from the corner of her road in order to drive her to the hotel in question. Climbing into his car, she settled down next to him and immediately closed her eyes.

"I guess you're not used to getting up at this time?" he mocked.

"Please don't speak, I had a rough night," she groaned, holding her head.

It was a very quiet fifteen-minute journey to the hotel.

"Ok, Carol, wake up, we're here." Carol opened her eyes and sat up in her seat. "Do you want me to come in with you?"

"Don't you think I'm capable of introducing myself? What sort of moron do you think I am?" she hissed.

Dropping her at the entrance, she jumped out of the car quickly; she did manage to thank him for the lift before slipping through the swivel doors.

Eight hours later, she was surprised to find him waiting for her in the lobby.

"Hi, how did it go?" he asked.

"I'm absolutely shattered – and, my feet! I think if I take my shoes off I'll never get them on again."

"Do you fancy going for a milkshake?"

"A milkshake sounds great, thanks."

***

"You didn't wait around the entire time for me to finish work, did you?" she queried, several minutes later, as she sucked slowly on her straw.

Joe laughed. "No, of course not."

"I'll catch the bus tomorrow."

"That's fine, I have classes all day tomorrow, anyway. Look Carol, I was wondering if I could take you out to dinner sometime?"

"I see! You get me a job, now you think I'm yours for the taking," she cried, jumping down from the

114

stool. "I'll find my own way home, thanks."

"No, please Carol, wait," he said, grabbing her arm, "that's not what I think at all. You must realise I fancied you from the first day we met. Look, we started off on the wrong foot then and it seems I've upset you again. Honestly, that wasn't my intention. I would simply like to take you to dinner, is that so bad?"

She climbed back onto the stool and crossed her long legs. "I guess not. I'm sorry; I can be a hothead at times. Ok, next Monday is my first day off, we could go out then?"

"Monday it is. I'll pick you up at seven."

Just after seven the following Monday, Joe pulled up outside Carol's house. Adjusting his attire, he rang the doorbell. He hoped the flowers he had bought at the last minute from the florist would be an acceptable bouquet for her mother. He had to wait for several agonising minutes before the door was finally opened. Carol's mother stood before him in shorts and a blouse that he could not help but notice gaped open slightly. Joe thought she was a lot younger than he had expected and had a look of Marilyn Monroe about her, which he found surprisingly arousing.

"Good evening, Mrs. Johnson."

"My name, young man, is not Mrs. Johnson; it's Mrs. Harris."

"Oh I'm sorry ... I didn't know. I'm Joe, Mrs. Harris, Joe Carter. I've come to pick up Carol, to take her to dinner."

"Carol? My Carol? Was she expecting you?"

"Yes, Mrs. Harris, we made a date for this

115

evening."

"Sorry young man, she's not here; haven't seen her all day," and with that she closed the door before he had a chance to say another word.

Climbing back into his car, he threw the flowers on to the back seat. What game was Carol playing? Did she think she could just toy with his feelings after he had admitted to her how he felt? He switched on the engine and put his foot down hard to the floor. He was angry with himself for caring too much about a girl who obviously did not give a shit about him.

Back in his bedroom, he locked the door firmly behind him before getting out the photos he had developed of Carol and covered half of his bed with the paper images. He could not hate her – how could he; he loved her too much. Lying naked in his bed with the pictures next to him, he imagined what it would be like to explore her body and to make love to her. Stifling his cries, he began touching himself, just as he had done so many times before. Completely satisfied, he drifted off into yet another disturbed sleep.

CHAPTER 12 – MOMMY DEAREST

Joe never did find out the reason Carol stood him up. How he wished he were not so obsessed with her and could get her out of his head so he could move on with his life. His dreams were definitely becoming more frequent. Dark dreams, where he would pick Carol up in his car and take her back to his bedroom. Once there, he would ply her with drinks with the sole intention of making love to her. Every time he got to the part where she started struggling, a faceless someone entered the room, whereupon he would wake up, sweating profusely and feeling disgusted with himself. What was wrong with him?

***

Frank was true to his word: the following summer, without any pomp and ceremony, he and Meme were married in a small chapel in the presence of Joe and just a few members of her family. Immediately it was over, Joe made his excuses about having to get to work and left. Frank did not put up any objections, believing his son's departure was probably best all round.

Joe was now working on the front desk of the Carter Premier Hotel in Miami, a good two hours commute from home; a position, if he were being honest, he was actually quite enjoying. By midday, the morning rush of people checking in and out had slowed, so he took the time to have a coffee break. With a steaming cup of black coffee and an iced doughnut in front of him, he began to study the faces of the people milling around. Rich people with money to burn, he thought, with wives who loved to spend and spend, just like the woman his father had married. How he hated her. He could not believe his father had been so naïve to have married someone with such low morals; who, Joe had not doubt, was only interested in one thing: his money.

He dreaded it now when his father went away on business trips, leaving him alone in the house with Meme, for she was always walking about half naked and tantalising him with her comments about how she could make a man of him. One night he even heard the handle of his bedroom door being tried; thank god he had locked it. What would she do, he wondered, if he actually took her up on her offer? Would she tell his father? No, of course not, she knew he would sling her out with the trash. Perhaps he should take her, just once, to give him a hold over her. He could imagine she was a hooker while they were doing it; after all, she dressed like one. He knew boys at college who bragged about visiting hookers, surely it would not be any different and it would not cost him a dime.

He was about to leave the cafe when he overheard two young Englishmen at the counter trying to pay. They seemed to be having trouble understanding the money in their hands, so he stepped up to see if he could be of any assistance. The two men in question turned out to be Teddy and Steve.

"We're fine," assured Steve, "this is not my first

visit to your country, but my friend here is a bit confused – but, like I said, we're fine."

"Ok," smiled Joe, "but if I can be of any help in future, you'll find me at the front desk."

Later that afternoon, Joe noticed the two young men again, apparently on their way out somewhere. Recognising a familiar face at the reception desk, Teddy made his way towards him.

"Hi," he began, "I just wanted to say thanks for earlier; my friend Steve was trying to teach me about the coins you have here – they are so different from the ones back home in England."

"No problem – as I said, I'm here to help."

Opening his wallet, Teddy produced a small leaflet. "We were thinking about going to this beach," he said, "do you know the best way to get there?"

Joe glanced at the piece of paper advertising South Beach. "Yes, it's quite easy. A taxi will only cost you about three dollars. I'll call one for you, if you'd like?"

"Thanks, we would appreciate that. It's Teddy, by the way, Teddy Macey," Teddy said, holding out his hand.

"Nice to meet you, Teddy," Joe reciprocated, taking a firm grip.

Just as Teddy was putting the leaflet back into his wallet, the picture of Mary fell onto the counter and Joe immediately picked it up.

"Is this your girlfriend?" he asked.

"No, it's my sister. Cute, isn't she?"

She certainly was, Joe thought; not only that, he instantly realised she resembled Carol and his mother. Three women all looking alike, what were the chances? Excited by this discovery, he decided there and then he had to get to know Teddy a lot more and, with any luck, his sister as well.

"Is she here with you on holiday?"

"No, she would have loved to have come, but I'm here with Steve and his parents."

"That's a shame, I would have liked to meet her. My name's Joe, by the way, my father just happens to own this hotel. I was thinking: I'm off tomorrow, if you like I could show you some fun places to go?"

"Yes, that would be great. I can't answer for Steve, of course, but I'd appreciate the tour, thanks."

Steve was waiting patiently at the entrance to the hotel. "Well, did you get directions?"

"Yes I did. He's really nice ... he's even offered to show me around."

Steve sighed. "I suppose I'll have to go along as well to keep an eye on you. Can't have you going off with strange men; your mum would never forgive me."

Two weeks later, Teddy and Steve's holiday came to an end and as the taxi drew away from the hotel entrance, Joe looked down triumphantly at the appropriated photo of Mary he was clutching in his hand.

***

The following year passed slowly. Of course, now there were three people living once more in the Carter house. Three people for Cassey to cook and clean for and, as far as Meme was concerned, anything else she commanded her to do. It was really infuriating to Joe, the way Meme talked down to the maid, as if she was a no-body. Then, one day, he found the waif crying in the kitchen.

"Cassey, whatever's the matter?" he asked sitting down beside her.

"It's nothing, Master Joseph, I'm just being silly."

Joe reached into his pocket and pulled out a Kleenex. "I know it's something, Cassey. Here, dry your eyes." Cassey took the tissue gratefully from his hand and dabbed at her cheeks.

"I can't tell you, Master Joseph. I'll lose my job."

"I would never let that happen Cassey; my mom brought you into this house because she thought the world of you, just as I do." Cassey's face lit up briefly. "I'm not leaving here until you tell me what's upset you."

Twisting the wet tissue between her fingers, she pursed her lips. "Mistress Carter ordered me to clear Miss Diana's room while she was out. She ordered me, Master Joseph, to throw everything out into the garbage."

Slamming his hand down on the kitchen table, Joe rose to his feet. Without uttering a word, he made his way out of the kitchen, through the hall and up the snaking stairs until he came to the door of his mother's room. He took the handle firmly in his right hand and turned it. It had always been an understanding between him and his father that, when they both felt ready, between them they would go through Diana's personal effects. Of course, the time just never seemed right and, for Joe, keeping the room as it was on the day she died had been a real comfort. When life seemed unbearable, he would sit in the chair by her bed, holding her precious shawl to

121

his face, close his eyes and inhale the now faint aroma that it yielded whilst visualising her still in the room.

Joe clenched his fists. Apart from the furniture, the room had been stripped of all his mother's belongings: her little bit of jewellery and her closets of clothes, everything was gone. There was nothing left to remind him of her. Even the pearl-handled gun Diana always kept close by her and the syringes used for her medication had disappeared from the bedside table. Leaving the room, he ran back down the stairs and outside to the back of the house. It was all there, bagged up and thrown into the garbage, just as Cassey had said. He clasped his hands at the back of his head and then, meticulously, he began pulling out every single bag before carrying them back into the house.

"Cassey?" he called out. "Cassey, can you help me?"

Between them, they very methodically put the room back to how it was.

"Mistress Carter will be so angry with me, Master Joseph," she whimpered.

"You leave your mistress to me; nothing's going to happen to you, do you understand?"

"Yes, Master Joseph, I understand."

***

It was getting dark when the headlights of Meme's car reflected off the fireplace wall. He had been waiting for hours in the den for this moment. He lifted the glass of cold beer to his lips and tipped it back until the only thing left were the droplets. He got to his feet and made his way into the hallway. He could hear her out on the porch outside trying to get her key in the lock. When at last the door swung open, she stumbled inside.

"Joe, how nice of you to wait up for your mom. Help me, will you? I've got bags, lots of bags."

He could tell straight away she had been drinking – whiskey was her tipple, doubles usually.

"Cassey!" she screamed. "Cassey, come here now!"

"Cassey has already gone to bed, I told her she could." Joe grinned. "How about having a drink with me in the den, you must be exhausted. I'll help you up with those bags in a minute."

Ordinarily, Joe would not be giving her the time of day, but this evening was different. This evening was payback time. Completely taken aback by his unfamiliar warm manner, she very willingly succumbed to his suggestion. Relaxing back on the enormous leather settee, she kicked off her high heels.

"Come and sit next to me darling, tell your mom what you've been up to. You know, you're looking a little peaky. Are you sure you're eating properly? We don't want your pa coming back to a sick boy now, do we?"

He began to pour whiskey from the decanter, before handing her the almost full glass. She patted the space next to her and he sat down.

"My, you're a handsome lad," she began, leaning in towards him, her hand stroking his face. "Is there a girl you've got your eye on? You can tell me, I won't be jealous, honest."

"No, there's no girl," he said, glancing up at the clock, "Christ, look at the time, I didn't realise how late it was. I have to be up early tomorrow, finish

123

your drink and I'll help you and your bags up to your room."

She needed his support as she mounted the flight of stairs. Progress was slow, but eventually they were standing outside her bedroom door. Inside, the four-poster bed, adorned with black silken sheets – her choice, naturally – lay ostentatiously as the centrepiece of the room.

"Is there anything else I can help you with?" he asked, as she eased herself onto the bed.

Grabbing at him, she caused him to lose his balance and land on top of her. Now face-to-face, she smiled.

"I think, young man, the time is right. You don't want to be a virgin forever, do you? Let me show you what it's like to be inside a real woman."

Slowly, she began to unbutton her silk blouse, exposing a white lacy bra.

"Unhook it for me darling, will you?" she encouraged, turning her back towards him. He had never seen a naked woman before. Of course, the girls on the beach wore very little, but he had never actually seen breasts or touched them – but he could not say that any more.

"Be gentle with me," she teased as he mounted her. The act was over in minutes.

"I have to say, Joe, you've got a lot of potential; if that was your first time I can't wait for the repeat performance," she coaxed, lying back on the pile of pillows; her dyed red hair splayed in all directions. "Look, I need a cigarette. I've left mine downstairs, be a love and get them for me, will you?"

He leaped up from the bed and glanced back at

her naked body – she made no effort to cover up and seemed to relish his staring eyes. Swiftly, he made his way not downstairs, but to his bedroom. Picking up his camera, which had laid patiently waiting for its part in his master plan, he returned and stood over the four-poster bed. She had not passed out yet, he had to be quick. He started clicking before she could comprehended what was happening, taking intimate pictures he hoped would put a stop to her manipulation of himself and Cassey.

"What are you doing, Joe darling? Do you have my cigarettes?" she whined, looking up at him through her drunken haze, smudged mascara making her appearance even more unpleasant than usual.

"Sorry, I couldn't find them, why don't you have a sleep, I want you to look your best tomorrow," he coaxed as he began fondling her body. Emitting a purr-like sound, she immediately turned onto her side and closed her eyes. That was exactly what he was waiting for. Nestling in behind her, he lifted his camera and clicked again and again. Satisfied, he eased himself off the bed, dressed and left the sleeping whore. Down in his darkroom, he locked the door behind him and began to work.

***

Meme was very late coming down the following morning; in fact, it was almost noon when he finally heard her voice demanding coffee. He had waited around the house for her appearance, not wanting Cassey to have to face her on her own.

"Joe, my darling boy, be a love and see what's

keeping that girl, will you? I've been calling her for ages; I think she must be deaf as well as stupid."

Joe came across Cassey cowering in the kitchen, whereupon he put his arm around her shoulders.

"Cassey, it's alright, you don't have to worry, just bring her the coffee and I'll take it from there."

"But Master Joseph, she'll be so angry when she finds out the room hasn't been cleared."

"Cassey, I told you to leave her to me," he repeated, "give me a few minutes to get back to her and then come in with the coffee."

Meme was waiting impatiently in the den when Joe re-joined her.

"Coffee won't be long; Cassey was in the middle of preparing dinner."

"Useless, that's what she is, absolutely bloody useless! Why your pa employed her in the first place, I'll never know."

Entering with coffee and a large slice of cake, Cassey put the tray down besides Meme, who immediately grabbed her arm.

"Well, did you carry out that little task I gave you yesterday? Is it all sorted?" she hissed, so close to her face that the poor maid feared she would pass out from the unpleasant stale odour being discharged from her mistress's mouth.

Cassey looked alarmed and glanced over at Joe, who rose to his feet.

"Cassey, you can go now."

"How dare you dismiss my maid!" she screamed, before turning back to stare at the poor young woman. "I asked you a question, girl?"

Struggling to find the words to reply, Cassey broke

126

from her grasp and fled from the room in tears.

Joe stood strong in front of his stepmother, stopping her from following.

"Just so you know, Meme, Cassey carried out your order to clear my mom's room and, just so you know, I've put it all back again and if you ever try anything like that again, I'll kill you."

"You'll kill me?" she roared, laughing in his face; not quite the response he was expecting. Narrowing her eyes she jabbed at him with her finger. "You're a joke. I know you go into Diana's room – I've watched you. You're a pathetic mommy's boy. I pity any woman who comes into your life because she will always be there, in your head and probably in your bed too."

The vein in his neck started throbbing; nevertheless, surprisingly, he managed to keep calm.

"Have you quite finished? Anyway, I was going to add that I want you to treat Cassey with the respect she deserves in future and to keep well away from me."

"I don't think you realise who you're talking to, young man: I'm the mistress of this household and don't you forget it! I will treat that maid anyway I like and, as for you, well, I've had better."

Trying to ignore her cutting remark, he picked up an envelope from the bookshelf.

"I didn't want to do this but you're forcing my hand. I don't think you were aware in your drunken stupor last night, but I took some excellent pictures of you and me in, let's say, some very compromising positions." He lifted the black and white photos from the packet and laid them out on the coffee table.

"You little shit!" she screamed, her face becoming flushed while her eyes widened in disbelief at the sight of the prints in front of her.

"Now, now, Stepmother dear, don't get upset. Naturally Pa would, I've no doubt, throw you out of the house if I were to show him these intimate pictures. As for me? Yes, he would be angry, but I'm his son – eventually he would forgive me. So, you see, as long as you promise to leave my mom's things alone in future and treat Cassey, as I said, with respect, no one else needs to be shown these pornographic shots, which I'm actually quite proud of. We're both quite photogenic, don't you think?"

"Bastard," she yelled. "Bloody bastard."

***

By the time Frank returned home, he had been away for almost a week and immediately he made it clear he was eager to speak to his son.

"Well, Joe my boy, how are things going at college? Do you think you'll pass your exams?" he asked as he lit up a cigarette.

"I think it's going ok Pa but, as I said from the start, I'm not sure it's what I want to do with my life."

Frank hesitated slightly before replying. "Yes, I remember and that's exactly why Meme and I have been talking about your future. We would like to suggest you go away for a while, say a year in Europe, where I've got a lot of contacts, to give you experience on how foreign hotels operate. Then, when you come back, if you still want to try other things I won't stand in your way. How does that sound?"

Joe noticed his father never actually looked him directly in the eyes while he was making his speech. Of course, he knew only too well where all this was coming from. He glanced over at Meme who had her head in a glamour magazine. Yes, he knew exactly where this suggestion to get rid of him for a while was coming from.

Later that same evening, he called round for Angel and told him about his father's plans.

"Wish I were in your shoes, going off to Europe, just think of all those horny women you'll meet."

"Believe me Angel, you wouldn't want to be in my shoes. I'm not really sure I want to go anyway, I hate it at home but …"

"But nothing, go man, enjoy."

"Anyone would think you want rid of me."

Rubbing his hands together, Angel cleared his throat. "Not exactly man … but I have got something to tell you. I've been putting it off, mainly because I know you're not going to like it. In fact, I wouldn't blame you if you wanted to punch me."

"Go on, it can't be that bad."

"Ok, I'll just come out with it. I'm dating Carol."

Joe eyeballed him in disbelief, rose and with three long strides reached the front door.

"Joe, I'm sorry man, really I am, but I've always fancied her too you know, and you have to admit you did have your chance with her …"

Joe turned and glared at his friend. "You're right, I do want to punch you, but I won't; you're not worth the effort."

***

Finding out his best friend was dating the girl of his dreams was the turning point in his decision to go to

Europe. Eventually, everything was sorted; his bags were packed and the itinerary for his trip agreed – however what he was most sad about was leaving Cheyenne. Arrangements had been made for a young lad, who already did odd jobs around the estate, to care for the mount whilst he was away, so at least Joe felt reasonably confident he was leaving him in safe hands.

In the end, it was Cassey who came to the airport to see him off, his father being too busy with work and Meme … well … apparently she had a hair appointment.

"Now, don't forget to write Master Joseph; I want to know all about your travels. Look, I hope you don't mind but I've brought you a little going away gift," she said, handing him a small parcel tied with a silver ribbon. "I'm not very good at wrapping parcels, I'm afraid," she added, blushing slightly.

"Cassey, you really shouldn't have spent your money on me, but thank you, thank you so much and, by the way, it's wrapped perfectly." He bent down and kissed her cheek softly. "Look, if Mistress Carter gives you any trouble, just let me know straight away, ok? I know precisely how to deal with her."

CHAPTER 13 – THE JOURNAL

Settling back in the first class cabin of the aircraft, Joe closed his eyes. With the roar of the engine ringing in his ears he contemplated, not for the first time, whether he was doing the right thing by backing down over this trip to Europe. His father and Meme had not won, even if they believed they had, for he still had no intention of working in the hotel industry no matter how many incentives were thrown at him. Nevertheless, even with all these family issues surrounding him, his innermost thoughts were still with Carol. His dark dreams were happening more and more frequently and, not only that, they were becoming more violent in nature – and, even more alarmingly, he now actually looked forward to falling asleep.

Remembering Cassey's gift, he opened his eyes and pulled at the ribbon – a journal bound in black leather. Moved by the thoughtfulness of its giver, he found a pen and began to write.

I have never kept a journal before, but I think I'm going to enjoy it. How I hated leaving Carol behind with my so-called friend. I'm praying that when I get back their relationship will have come to an end and I can take my rightful place by her side. As for my stepmother, I hope she rots in hell ...

It's the end of my first day in London; I'm exhausted with the flight and the time change. I had a meal with Mary and Teddy here in my hotel room this evening. Mary seems very innocent and much younger than her years. She definitely looks a lot like Mom and Carol and I'm sure if I play my cards right she will eventually surrender to my charms. Is she a substitute Carol? Yes, that's exactly how I see her. I'm going to play it cool with Mary, nurture her feelings before making my move. I think telling Carol I fancied her right at the beginning gave her the upper hand ...

Well, that was an unfortunate moment. Why would Teddy think I was gay? It's really upset me. More than that, my beautiful Mary was not with him. I've had the pictures developed I've taken of her; there are some lovely shots. I will lay them out tonight on my bed; I hope Carol won't be jealous. Mary's begun to appear in my dark dreams. I do things to her I wouldn't do to Carol. I don't think I want to hurt her but, in my dreams, the more she struggles the more I like it ...

Tonight was my last evening in London and I spent it with Mary – sweet, innocent Mary. I must say she looked very sexy in her new dress. This was the first time we've had any alone time together, I did manage a kiss, although I wanted much more. Next time, yes, I've made up my mind there will definitely be a next time ...

France was a great experience, but exhausting, I hardly had any time to myself. Angel was right; I've had women of all ages falling at my feet, especially when they find out I'm the son of a multimillionaire. Arrived in Switzerland this morning, beautiful view from my window of the snow-covered mountains. Will have to have a go at skiing while I'm here ...

What's wrong with me? When I got back to my room this evening, this blonde who's been following me around since I got here was waiting outside my door. Wow, she's gorgeous, always wearing tight-fitting clothes and legs that go on forever. Well, there she was, apparently locked out of her apartment. She said she didn't want to bother the night staff and could she sleep in my room ... and what was my reply? I told her I'd go down to reception for her key. Why? I repeat, what's wrong with me? I hate to think it could be true, but was my bitch of a stepmother right? Do I only want women who look like my mom in my bed? Am I sick?

I flew back to London this morning. Dinner with Mary and Teddy – must remember Edward not Teddy. Mary looked more adorable than I recall. Fortunately, we had a few minutes together before Edward arrived. How I wanted her to stay with me tonight. We could have made love in my king-sized bed, but still she resists me. However, the solution suddenly presented itself; her bag was open and I took her purse. I had to do it, didn't I?

I'm on the plane home at last. This morning I have to admit is a bit of a blur. I remember Mary arriving at my hotel room looking for her purse. We kissed and I told her I wanted more, and then – now this is where I'm confused. It was as if I was playing out part of my dark dreams. I heard myself asking her to marry me, but in my head I was asking Carol. It was Carol who I lift up in my arms and carried to my bed. It was Carol who laid naked on the sheets and who was muttering cries of ecstasy as I touched her. It was Carol who I made love to. It was Carol with whom I talked of wedding plans. It was Carol who I promised to call. It was Carol who I left at the station – but I realised too late, she wasn't Carol, was she? What's wrong with me?

CHAPTER 14 – REVENGE IS SWEET

Home at last, finally, Joe felt he could relax. As his father's chauffeur turned the car left through the electric-gated entrance into Fouracres, the short drive to the house had begun. With his heart pounding hard in his chest, he inhaled the view of the tree- and shrub-filled landscape he had missed over the year. A flat, dry land of white sandy soil from which, when the wind blew, fine grains settled everywhere possible on your body – of course, he was used to that. It was his homeland, exactly where he wanted to be, no matter what obstacles were thrown at him by his father and stepmother. He had been fantasising about this moment for weeks and, very soon, he would be riding his beloved Cheyenne again along the beach, with the sun beating down relentlessly on his back.

The house was quiet. He knew his father was away in California; thankfully, there seemed to be no sign of Meme either. He left his suitcases at the bottom of the stairs and headed for the kitchen. Cassey, with her back to him, was standing at the sink. He crept up behind her and put his hand on her shoulder. Turning around, she screamed in sheer delight at the very sight of him.

"Master Joseph, oh, I didn't know you were coming home today, no one told me. Oh, Master Joseph it's so wonderful to see you again."

"It's good to see you too, Cassey. I don't suppose there's any chance of a glass of iced tea?" he beamed, as he pulled out a chair and sat down at the kitchen table. "By the way, the journal was a brilliant gift, thanks; I've just about managed to write something in it every week."

Lifting a large jug of iced tea from the fridge, she poured out two glasses and handed him one.

"I'm glad you liked it, I've kept a journal myself since I've lived here. Did you have a good time in Europe? What were the people like? Did you take lots of pictures? I would really like to see them."

"One question at a time, Cassey. First, how have you been? And what have you done with the old witch, my stepmother?"

Cassey looked down at her glass and cooled her hands on its cold exterior.

"Mistress Carter went to visit her sister in Georgia; not sure when she'll be home. She doesn't tell me about her comings and goings, she says she doesn't to keep me on my toes."

"I see, let's hope she's away for a long time then. Well, I think I'll take my bags up to my room, have a shower and then go out and see Cheyenne. I hope he's missed me as much as I've missed him."

Cassey's face dropped and tears began to well in her eyes as she clasped her hands tightly together.

"Oh, Master Joseph, haven't they told you?"

"Told me? Told me what? Cassey, you're scaring me, has something happened to Cheyenne?"

Cassey's lower lip began to tremble. "When I got back from the airport, the day you left, the trucks were already here."

"Trucks? Cassey, what are you talking about?"

"I don't think the Master knew of her plans; there

was a terrible row when he came back and found out but, of course, by then it was too late."

"Too late for what, Cassey? Please … tell me!"

Cassey lifted her eyes up towards him knowing the pain she was about to impart to the young man so dear to her heart.

"She got the men to pull down the barn, Master Joseph, after they took Cheyenne away. Mistress Carter said the vet told her he was old and had to be put down. She had him killed Master Joseph; she killed Miss Diana's horse."

Joe's haunting howl of agonising grief echoed throughout the house. With a look of a demented soul, he leapt for the back door, almost taking if off its hinges as he stormed through it. Running towards the part of the estate where the barn had once stood, he stopped dead in his tracks for now, instead of the barn his mother had had built all those years ago, a large swimming pool gleamed in the heat of the day.

"Cheyenne!" he cried, looking to the heavens, "I'm so sorry!"

Sinking to the dusty ground, he lay there for several minutes in agony of the destruction of his friend. Then, hearing footsteps approaching from behind, he looked up slowly and glared into the eyes of the perpetrator.

"Joe, it's so nice to see you again, your pa will be sorry not to have been here, although he's due home tomorrow apparently. Fancy a swim?"

Meme stood before him with a triumphant smile that he just wanted to wipe off her face. Without a word, he rose to his feet and walked back towards the house.

"So much nicer, don't you think," she called out after him, "to have a pool rather than that smelly creature about the place; never did like horses."

***

Joe stayed in his room for the rest of the day, planning his revenge. Oh yes, he would have his revenge.

Before the sun had risen in the cloudless sky the following day, he made his way down to his studio and darkroom. There it was, exactly where he had left it, the metal box housing bottles of poisoned chemicals. Donning a pair of rubber gloves for protection, he unlocked the box carefully and removed the smallest bottle containing cyanide. Holding the syringe he had retrieved from his mother's room, he managed to extract the entire liquid. Moving to his workbench, he began to inject the European cigarettes, and then the continental chocolates, with the poisonous solution – surprise gifts for his father and Meme. Gratified by his endeavours, he divided the cigarettes evenly between two silver cases and rewrapped the chocolates. Bagging up all incriminating evidence into a backpack, he locked the door behind him and went up to the kitchen in search of Cassey.

There she was, slaving over the stove as usual, preparing breakfast.

"Morning Cassey, mmm, those biscuits smell good."

"Oh, morning, Master Joseph. My, you're up early, do you want your breakfast now?"

"Just coffee and a couple of your biscuits would be great, thanks. Look, I'm going away for a few days, I can't bear being in the house with my stepmother after what she did to Cheyenne. It's your day off, isn't it? Can I drive you anywhere?"

"Oh, I haven't anything planned, Master Joseph. I just thought I'd catch up on my reading in my room."

Joe studied her closely. "You look worn out, when was the last time you had a vacation?"

"Vacation? I had a couple of days with my friend Peggy last Christmas."

"You need a proper break, starting today. I don't want any arguments, contact your friend Peggy and tell her you've a week's vacation booked."

"Oh no, honestly Master Joseph, I couldn't. The Master wouldn't agree at such short notice, and anyway, I can't really afford it at the moment."

"You leave my pa to me, I'll ring him now and, as for the money, I think you deserve some time off on the Carter family. Go on, go and get packed while I make a few phone calls."

Caught up in a whirl of excitement, Cassey obeyed his instructions and ran to her suite of rooms, adjoining the kitchen, in order to start packing.

An hour later, Joe sat at the table drumming his fingers, waiting for her return. When she did, he got to his feet immediately, impatient to be away.

"Right, that's all done. You're booked into one of our better hotels in Miami; I've told them you're a special guest. If your friend Peggy can get the time off they will accommodate her too."

"Oh thank you, Master Joseph, I don't know how I will ever repay you."

"Just go and have a great time. I managed to contact my pa, by the way," he lied, "he agreed to you having leave and even added it was one of my better ideas."

After loading Joe's car at the back of the house, they made their exit along the driveway. Fortunately, upstairs Meme was still deep in sleep, the result of yet another drunken evening. The two escapees headed east along the highway, now congested with the morning commute into work. After two hours, they arrived at the beachfront hotel.

"Oh, it looks lovely Master Joseph, thank you again. Where are you off to, by the way?"

"Nowhere in particular, I'll just drive for a while and book into a motel somewhere."

A deep frown crossed her face.

"Now, don't you worry about me; I'll be ok. I just need some time on my own that's all."

Joe surveyed Cassey with some relief, as she carried her suitcase through the hotel door. Re-entering the stream of traffic, he followed the signs west and headed back towards home. Right, now to find some sleazy motel.

It was mid-morning by the time he pulled into Pete's Motel. The woman on reception hardly glanced up at him as he began to sign his name in the motel's register.

"How long do you think you'll be with us?" she asked, finally putting down the newspaper she had been reading. Looking up at him, she almost choked on her gum as she gazed dreamily into Joe's handsome face.

"Not too sure, certainly a couple of days."

"Lucky me ... here's the key to number twelve," she said, leaning over the desk so far that Joe could see down the front of her blouse, "if you need anything, anything at all, I'm here to help. It's Estelle, by the way, my mother was French."

"Right, I bet she was a beautiful woman, Estelle. Thanks anyway, but I'm in need of peace and quiet, so I would appreciate not being disturbed for the entire time I'm here."

"Well, if you're sure," she said, glancing down at the registry book. "It's such a shame that a young man like you, Joe Carter, should be on his own."

"I can assure you, it's what I want. So, where's this room?"

"It's on your left as you go out of here. I'll show you if you like?"

"No, that's fine, I'm sure I can find it."

The room, not surprisingly, was sparsely decorated with a double bed and side table housing a lamp, topped with a slightly stained shade. Beneath the only window in the place stood an ancient chest of drawers that looked like it could have been around in the civil war. A handle-less door led into a shabby shower and toilet. It would do for what he had planned.

***

Dusk was already falling when he dressed himself in the olive green overalls and baseball hat he had uncovered in the basement at home. Carrying a backpack and his mother's pearl-handled gun deep in his pocket, he snuck out of the room and started walking towards the highway. It did not take him long to flag down a truck, whose driver seemed only too grateful for his company and the chance of a conversation, not that Joe was in the mood for a chat. About a mile from home, he asked the driver to drop him off outside a retail park, making the excuse he was meeting a friend. As the truck drew away, he began the final stretch on foot.

Now the electric gates loomed large in front of him. Removing the remote control from his backpack, with one click they began to open with a whining clatter, enabling him to slip through easily. Running hard towards the house, darting amongst the evening shadows, he stopped a few feet away, removed his outer clothing and shoved them into the backpack before hurling the bag into the bushes. Entering the house from the kitchen door, he grabbed a cold beer to calm his nerves. Right, he was more than ready. Frank was in the hall looking through his mail when he first caught sight of him.

"Joe, my boy, welcome home. I was just coming to find you, Meme said you haven't been out of your room all day."

"Yes, that's right Pa, I've been suffering from jet lag."

"Well, it's great that you're up and about at last. How did you find your time in Europe? I've had some great feedback from the hotels you've worked in; nothing but praise. I can't tell you how proud I am."

Joe scrutinized him closely: the well renowned Frank Carter, the man who once told him how much he loved his mother, had brought evil into their house in the form of his lover. What did this make his father? For it was he who had allowed her to live under the same roof and sleep beside him in the same bed in which his beloved mother had once lain. Yes, his father was just as guilty. In fact, thinking about it, it was his fault entirely that Cheyenne was dead. Neither he nor Meme deserved to live a moment longer.

"Nice to see you too, Pa. Yes, I had a good time, even brought you a few little gifts back. I'll go and get them, perhaps we could all have a drink in the den to celebrate my return?"

"Good idea, my boy, I'll go and find Meme, I know she's as excited as I am at having you home."

Entering the den several minutes later, Joe was just in time to hear Meme muttering something about how inconvenient it was that it was Cassey's day off.

"Everyone surely is entitled to time off," Joe interjected, as he stepped through the door. "I have to say, in Europe the staff have more vacation time than our employees do here."

"Don't go shouting that too loudly my boy; that sort of talk will cost us money. Now, where are these gifts you mentioned?"

Joe reached into a duty-free bag. "Right, there's two each; I wanted to keep it fair. It doesn't matter which you open first."

Eagerly, Frank and Meme ripped at the paper. "A cigarette case with my initials. A lovely thought, thank you my boy, and Swiss chocolates ... can't wait to taste those."

"Oh and I've got the same – you've even put in some European cigarettes for us to try, very thoughtful, Joe," exclaimed Meme, rather taken aback by his gesture.

"Well, I'm pleased you like them. What do you want to try first, the cigarettes or the chocolates?"

"I could really do with that drink first," Frank replied. "Then I want to hear everything about your trip." He moved to the bar and began pouring out three whiskeys, at the same time Meme took out her lighter and lit one of the cigarettes. "I think I'll join you darling; hand me your lighter, I've left mine upstairs."

Meme looked down at the burning cigarette between her fingers. "It's much stronger than the ones I usually smoke ... what do you think, Frank?"

Frank inhaled hard on the one he had lit. "Yes, it's definitely a bit stronger, but I like it."

Waiting patiently for a reaction from his endeavours, Joe could not help the smirk of satisfaction that erupted across his face. "Do you fancy a chocolate? They are really delicious, believe me; you won't be able to stop at just one."

Meme was the first to place one in her mouth. How long, Joe contemplated, would the poison take to kill them? Would it be instant or would there be hours of excruciating pain? He hoped for the latter.

"You're right Joe, they are yummy, although they do have a slight aftertaste. Frank, you try one."

After eating several pieces of the sweet confectionery, it was Meme who was the first to experience symptoms. Within minutes, she was complaining of a headache and dizziness and then the vomiting started.

"What's happening, Frank? I suddenly feel really ill. Joe, ring for the doctor! I feel too weak to walk.

Joe, don't just sit there with a grin on your face, your pa and I need a bloody doctor!"

Joe sat back on the couch and took a lingering sip from his glass.

"Oh dear, look at the two of you. Pa, on the positive side, at least you're confined to your favourite chair."

"Joe, what the hell have you done?" Frank whispered, his breathing becoming more rapid.

Finally, jumping to his feet, Joe began to pace the room.

"Do you honestly think I would accept the killing of an innocent horse? Oh yes, Stepmother dear, I've had the last laugh. Look at you crawling on the floor, like the low life creature you are, you'll get your dress even dirtier. Let me help you into a chair." He turned to his father. "Pa, you're just as much to blame; I couldn't let you live either, could I? Have you any idea of the true nature of this bitch of a woman you married? I've had her Pa, in your bed. She's been after me since that day you got engaged. Don't look so shocked Pa, she's trash and now, like you, she stinks of vomit."

Clawing at their throats and with a final gasp, it was all over.

"Oh, how disappointing, I had hoped your agony was going on for a little bit longer. No matter."

He positioned them both in their chairs, just as if they had simply fallen asleep, before packing away the poisoned cigarettes and chocolates.

"Now for my pièce-de-résistance," he sneered.

He began to pour the whisky slowly into their mouths, although naturally most of it ended up over

145

their clothing, which is exactly what he wanted to happen. Placing a wastepaper bin by Meme's chair, he scrunched up several magazines and newspapers before lighting one of her own cigarettes. Inserting it between her fingers, he watched as its ash made its descent into the bin below, followed in due course by the filter. As the paper began to smoulder, he glanced down at their distorted faces and anticipated how long it would take for their bodies to burn.

"I hope you two enjoy hell, because I've no doubt that's where you're headed."

With the flames now taking hold, he left the den behind and made his way back outside. Retrieving the bag of clothes from beneath the shrubbery, he began to run back towards the gates.

He had to walk for several miles before a truck driver offered him a lift and it was just after midnight when he arrived back at Pete's Motel. He showered, prior to climbing into bed, and opened his journal at the last entry before picking up his pen.

I will never forget you, Cheyenne. Revenge, they say, is sweet. R.I.P. my dear friend.

CHAPTER 15 – THE FALLOUT

Joe rose early the next morning, packed everything that would tie him to the murders into his backpack, except for the chocolates (no, for some reason he decided to hang on to those for the time being) and loaded his car before handing his key into reception.

"I'm going for breakfast," he told the elderly man behind the desk, "can you recommend anywhere?"

"You'll find The Gator Café before you get back to the highway, tell them Pete sent you."

The Gator Café was certainly a good place to dine if you wanted to be noticed. He ordered a full breakfast of eggs, bacon and hash browns, swigging it all down with several cups of coffee. Anyone watching him would think he was a young man without a care in the world, certainly not a cold-blooded killer. He chatted away happily to other diners and even tipped the waitress well before he left, so she would remember him. With a full belly, he set off south toward the Everglades. He had always loved the mystique of this region as a child. Enjoyed the days when his father would load up the station wagon and together they would drive to the heart of the wetlands, hire a speedboat and go fishing.

Of course, that was another life entirely; one he could now only barely remember. Parking his car in a remote area, he removed the backpack from the trunk. Wearing sunglasses and a baseball hat, he began to hike through the overgrown vegetation towards a lake of stagnating water, delighting in the sights and sounds of the undisturbed nature surrounding him. He took hold of the backpack and, with all his might, threw the bag as far as he could into the swamp and watched with little emotion at the ripple it caused before sinking without trace. Right, time to get back to the motel and wait for the news.

***

It was the sound of the motel owner, Pete, pounding on his door that woke Joe from his surprisingly deep slumber.

"Sorry to disturb you, but are you the son of Frank Carter, the hotel owner?"

"Yes, what's all this about?" asked Joe, looking at the man through blurry eyes.

"I've just heard on the radio there's been a fire at your home and they're asking if anyone had seen you or any members of your family."

"Oh Christ, no! Did they say … is anyone hurt?"

"Not sure, all I heard was they had managed to put out the fire before it had done too much damage."

"I see. Ok, I'll get my things together. Thanks."

***

The grounds of the mansion were a hive of activity when he arrived back at Fouracres. Several fire trucks and police cars were jamming the driveway, which had been cordoned off by tape to prevent prying eyes from getting any closer to the house. Joe got out of his car and stared at the sight in front of him. From the outside, it looked as if the entire right-hand side of the property, which included the den and his

148

father's study, had been totally destroyed. He started to make his way towards the front door, but was immediately stopped from going any further by a towering police sergeant.

"Sorry sir, it's not advisable to go inside."

"Do you know who I am? I'm Joe Carter, I think my pa might have been in there," Joe cried as he tried to push past.

"Oh, yes sir, I know who you are. I'm so sorry you've come home to this. The fire service are doing their checks at the moment, we'll let you know if they find anything."

"What do you mean, find anything? Do you mean a body?" Joe screamed.

"Calm yourself, sir, nothing's certain yet. If you go and sit in my car, one of my officers will look after you, we'll give you any information as soon as we have it."

It was a long wait. Eventually, the fire chief emerged from the building, his face blackened by smoke. He removed his helmet before making his way purposefully towards Joe.

"Mr. Carter? I'm Fire Chief Fensome. I understand you told the police sergeant you think your father was in the house? Was anyone else home, as far as you know?"

"I stayed at a motel last night and our maid is on vacation, but my pa and my stepmother should have been here. Have you found them? Are they dead?"

"Yes, I'm sorry, there's no easy way to tell you, but we've uncovered two bodies."

Joe put his head in his hands and began to wail. "Oh please no, Pa ... I love you! Please say it isn't true."

"I do appreciate that this is hard for you to take in and I hate to ask you under such difficult circumstances," the fire chief continued, "but we need you to help us to identify them. They were both wearing jewellery; if you could simply say the pieces belonged to your parents that should be sufficient at this juncture."

"How burned are they? I really don't think I can look. He was my pa, I loved him, I want to remember him as he was, not a pile of ash." Joe was certainly putting on a good display of grief.

"I'll not ask you to look at the bodies, sir, because yes, sadly, they are – I'm afraid - unrecognisable."

Forced tears were now staining Joe's cheeks.

"How do you think it happened, Chief Fensome?" he asked.

"It's too early to say for definite, sir, but in my experience, by the way the bodies were sitting in the chairs, perhaps one of them was smoking before falling asleep."

"I see, yes, that makes sense, they were both heavy smokers," replied Joe, wiping his eyes. "Ok, so where's this jewellery you were talking about?"

***

Two months later and the rebuilding of the mansion was well under way. However, its restoration was not the only major development taking place, Joe decided to have the builders fill in Meme's swimming pool at the same time. Its eradication from his sight bringing him even more satisfaction.

The tabloids had been full of stories of the Carter Empire over the past weeks and, to be truthful, Joe was sick and tired with the whole matter. The police had interviewed both him and Cassey in depth on more than one occasion and, fortunately for Joe, in the end they seemed to be satisfied with both their alibis. A verdict of misadventure was finally delivered on Frank and Meme's deaths, so now – believing he had got away with murder – Joe could finally move on with his life.

Then, one stormy evening, when Joe was alone in the house, he was forced to answer the intercom from the front gate to a certain someone who, as it turned out, had blackmail on her mind.

"Yes?" Joe answered curtly.

"Package for Mr. Carter," the female voice informed him.

Ten minutes later, he opened the door to a very bedraggled visitor.

"What a night, we've not had a storm like this for a long time, the roads are already beginning to flood. Aren't you going to let me in?"

"Excuse me? Didn't you say something about a package? If not, I think you've got the wrong house."

"Oh no, Joe Carter, I've got the right house. Don't you remember me? It's Estelle from Pete's Motel, I've come for a little chat."

"I really don't think you and I have got anything to chat about," replied Joe, trying to close the door as Estelle placed her body between it and the frame.

"I beg to differ. That night you stayed at the motel, I happened to see you sneaking out the back way and followed you as far as the highway. I saw you getting a lift from that truck driver which I thought strange at the time, mainly because your car was still parked in the motel car park. It crossed my mind that you were up to no good. Do you want to prove me wrong?"

Joe stepped aside, allowing the drenched woman to enter the hallway.

"What are you trying to accuse me of?" he asked.

"Accuse you? Let's see, I read the police report today, in which you stated you were asleep in your motel room on the night of the fire. Well, I know and you know that that was a lie." She took off her wet coat and started looking around her. "What a nice place you have here, it must be worth millions. Am I right?"

"I'm taking it you want money? How much to keep your mouth shut?" He could feel his anger mounting. How dare this whore come into his house and make demands.

"Oh dear, you sound upset. What's a few dollars when you've got all this? Let me see, one million would get me away from here and allow me to set up my own beauty business. Yes, one million sounds a good starting point. There's no rush; by the end of the week will be fine. For now, how about offering me something to eat, I'm famished." She looked at him with desire in her eyes, for a second she reminded him of Meme. "You know something? I'm going to call you Joe; after all, we are going to be seeing a lot of each other in the future, we may even become close friends, even lovers."

Not giving credence to her suggestion, he asked, "How did you get here? I didn't hear a car."

"I was driving my old wreck of a wagon, but it broke down several miles away. I managed to flag down a cab and the driver dropped me off at the entrance. I hadn't realised how long your drive was. Look, I tore my pantyhose on one of your bloody bushes." She hoisted up her skirt. "Do you like what you see, Joe? I can go higher if you want me to."

"I'm sure you can, but didn't you say you were hungry? First things first, the kitchen's through there," he pointed out, directing her gaze towards the kitchen door.

Managing to find a frying pan, Joe made them both a grilled cheese sandwich, which was followed by a large slice of Cassey's homemade apple pie.

"Mm that was delicious; your maid's a very good cook."

"Yes, she is, in fact I don't know what I'd do without her. Coffee?"

"That would round it off nicely. Perhaps we could take it up to your bedroom, I could do with a lie down?" she mused, placing her hand on his arm.

Repelled by her touch, he leapt to his feet. "I'll put the coffee on and then I've an added little treat in store; I'll just go and get them."

"Them? Oh, I hope you're not going to spoil me."

Joe returned to the kitchen moments later carrying a small box.

"I brought these back from Switzerland; the Swiss are famous for their chocolates, you know," he said, handing her the opened container.

"Lovely, I must admit I'm a bit of a chocoholic."

Joe watched with some satisfaction as she began stuffing them one by one, in a rather unladylike fashion, into her mouth, just as the smell of the percolated coffee was beginning to hit his nostrils.

"Do you take sugar?" he asked, as Estelle clutched at her throat. "No? Ok. I do, always have done. Oh, you poor girl, you look a little off-colour, perhaps I had better drive you home. Let me get your coat."

In silence, with his help, she managed – with great difficultly to put her arms in the sleeves before collapsing in a heap on the kitchen floor. Joe's mind was racing with what he needed to do next. Running upstairs, he found an old wooden chest and brought it down to the kitchen. He glared down at the rapidly dying woman.

"Stupid bitch. Look where your greed has got you."

Lifting up her now lifeless body, he placed it inside the chest and closed the lid, before making his way outside. Backing his father's old station wagon out of the garage with the relentless rain hammering hard on the windscreen, he parked the vehicle in front of the back door. The chest proved to be more of a challenge with a body inside; nevertheless, he managed to drag it to the rear of the car and, with a huge effort, placed it inside. With the storm still raging, he deemed it too treacherous to drive anywhere for the time being; he had no choice but to wait a few hours until it subsided.

**

The ringing of the phone by his bed woke him from his slumber several hours later.

"Master Joseph, it's Cassey, I'm sorry to wake you but I thought you'd be worried. I couldn't ring earlier because the phone lines were down and I couldn't get home because the weather was too awful, but I'll be on my way soon."

Christ, how could he have forgotten about Cassey?

"Cassey, oh don't worry about that – take your time, the roads will be too dangerous to travel on for hours yet; spend some time with your friends and I'll see you later this evening."

"Are you sure, Master Joseph? That's really nice of you."

"No problem, Cassey," he said before replacing the receiver.

Right, he had to get up and get rid of the body. He had had time to mull over his options during the night and there was no doubt in his mind that another trip to the Everglades was the answer. The roads were certainly more difficult to manoeuvre after the rains but, in due course, just as the sun began to rise in the sky, he found himself in the heart of the swamps. Driving to the most inhospitable area he could get to, he stopped the station wagon and dragged the chest out of the back. Opening the lid, he recoiled from the smell that wafted from its interior. He had no choice, of course, but to remove the rapidly decaying body. Struggling to walk through the tall grasses and peaty soil, he arrived at the nearest area of water inhabited by angry swarms of mosquitos hungry for animal or human blood. With all the strength he could muster, he tossed the corpse in as far as he could. Almost immediately, he heard a splash from the water's edge and, with surprising speed, a large alligator appeared and pulled the cadaver below the water line with its powerful jaws, twisting and thrashing about in the murky water, until it disappeared from his sight forever.

***

In the grounds of Fouracres, the dark grey smoke from the burning wooden chest lifted high into the sky. Poking at the fire, Joe watched the intense flames with some trepidation as to whether there were any more would-be blackmailers out there determined to bring him down, or was Estelle the only hiccup to his killings?

CHAPTER 16 – OLD FRIENDS

Waking in a sweat from yet another dark dream, Joe rose from his bed. His head was throbbing as he staggered towards his en-suite. Stepping into the shower cubicle, he turned the dial, instantly relishing the cleansing sensation the cascading water was having on his body. It had been several days now since he had disposed of Estelle and, as yet, there had been nothing on the media about a missing woman. Why should there be? She was an adult, so unless someone reported her missing there was no evidence to show a crime had been committed. Certainly, thanks to the alligator, there was no body to be discovered. Feeling revitalised, he dressed and made his way downstairs, only to be confronted by Cassey.

"Master Joseph, I've just had to open the gates to a police lieutenant, he said he wants to talk to you about a missing woman."

Alarm bells began to ring in his head, just as the sound of the doorbell reverberated through the house.

"Show him into the living room Cassey, and could you bring us a pot of coffee, please?"

Minutes later, a tall, slightly overweight detective with greying, greased back hair, bounded through the door.

"Mr. Carter," he began, his hand extended in greeting. "I'm Lieutenant Garcia, we met briefly when I was investigating the fire here."

"Oh yes, lieutenant, I vaguely remember you. How

can I help?"

The lieutenant took out his notebook. "We have had a report of a missing woman ... an Estelle Ward. She worked at Pete's motel, where you stayed a few months ago. Her abandoned car was found a few miles from here and a cab driver we've interviewed says he dropped her off at your gates."

"I see, when was this?"

"The night of the storm, were you at home then?"

"Yes, I think I was ... Cassey, my maid, was stranded at a friend's because of the weather, so I was alone."

"I see, so did you see this woman?"

"No lieutenant, I didn't. Oh yes, I remember now, I was working in my studio in the basement most of the day and part of the night. You can't hear the buzzer from the gate from down there since the fire mucked up the system, so I'm sorry, but I can't help you, presumably if she didn't get an answer she went away again."

"I see. Well, would you have any idea why Estelle would want to see you?"

Joe looked ponderous. "No lieutenant, no idea at all. I hardly spoke to the woman when I was staying there."

"I see, well that certainly is a mystery, sir. Why would a woman who hardly knew you drive her car all the way out here, and then pay for a cab to bring her to your house after hers had broken down? I mean, I would have thought that all she would have wanted to do was to get home. Very strange."

"Yes lieutenant, I agree with you, it is very strange." Joe looked up as Cassey entered. "Would you like coffee, lieutenant?"

"Yes, thank you sir, and I would also like a private word with your maid, if that's possible?"

"Of course. You can talk in here; I've got things to do. Cassey, will you let the lieutenant out when you've finished?" With those words, Joe got to his feet and left the room, somewhat relieved that the lieutenant seemed to have no more questions for him to answer.

Several days later, he was sitting down watching the television when a news report caught his attention.

'Earlier this evening, a local cab driver, whose name has not yet been released, was arrested and charged with the murder of Estelle Ward. Although her body has not been found, the police believe they have enough evidence for a conviction.'

Joe sat back in his chair and relaxed before pouring himself a stiff drink, confident now that that tiresome matter was over and done with.

***

It was November and the building works on Fouracres were nearly finished; there was just the small matter of sorting out the fate of the Carter hotels. Naturally, Frank had left Joe everything in his will, but what Joe wanted more than anything was to be rid of any physical involvement in the company and put his endeavours into starting up his own photography business to enable him follow in his mother's footsteps.

Nevertheless, understandably, the Carter Empire needed a figurehead, a leader, and with Joe having no interest in filling the position, decisions had to be made. Following an emergency board meeting in Miami, he proposed and it was passed unanimously by the board of directors and shareholders, that Frank's former right-hand man, Marcus Parmenter, be appointed Chief Executive Officer, leaving Joe at last free to do his own thing.

With the festive season looming fast, instead of partying and generally enjoying himself, as most young men of his age were doing, Joe was becoming a bit of a recluse, spending most of his time down in his studio and darkroom. He always kept both rooms, securely locked from prying eyes; even Cassey was not permitted to enter his private place, whose once bare walls were now covered in pictures of his beloved Carol. Since his return home from Europe, he had not even spoken to Angel, his former best friend, although he had heard through the grapevine that he and Carol were still going together, and this knowledge did not help his mood. With his mind continuing to play tricks on him, disturbed by everything that had happened over the past few months, he dipped in and out of the world of fantasy.

In his state of delusion, he began to truly believe he and Carol were getting married and even managed to develop pictures of them together as a couple. He started to organise the wedding, making lists of people to invite, designing wedding invitations, cutting out brides and bridesmaids dresses from magazines – in fact, troublingly, he planned everything down to the smallest detail.

It was early afternoon on Christmas Eve 1972 and he was steaming drunk. Cassey was out doing last-minute shopping and he was at home alone. He put on some music. Loud dancing music.

"What a wonderful day for a wedding," he cried, as he spun around with his arms splayed high in the

air. "I must share this wonderful day with a friend."
He started to dial.

"Edward, how great to hear your voice; it's Joe,
Joe Carter."

"Hi Joe, we've been worried about you! We're so
sorry about what happened to your parents, how are
you keeping?"

"Yes, their deaths were tragic, absolutely tragic, but
I'm holding up. I'm sorry I've not been in touch, only
I've had a lot to sort out with the business, you know
how it is. Look, the reason I'm calling is because I'm
about to get married, can you believe that, Joe Carter
is going to be a married man. Oh sorry, got to go,
give my love to Mary."

When Cassey came home later that day, she found
Joe passed out on the floor of the hallway.

"Master Joseph? Master Joseph, can you hear me?
It's Cassey, you have to get up."

"Cassey? Is that really you? Oh Cassey, you're the
only one who cares about me."

"Yes, Master Joseph, it's me, you have to get up
and get yourself to bed; it'll be Christmas day in a
couple of hours."

"Oh Cassey, I do love you," he said, manoeuvring
himself to a sitting position.

Cassey blushed at his words. "And I love you too,
Master Joseph, now come on, get to your feet, I'll put
a pot of coffee on and bring you a cup when you're in
bed."

"Do you want to join me, Cassey?"

"Now Master Joseph, I know it's the drink talking.
I'll forget you said that and you will have done, by the
morning. Go on, up you go."

***

A very sorry looking Joe joined Cassey in the kitchen

the following day.

"Happy Christmas, Master Joseph, how's the head?"

"Oh Cassey, I feel a herd of cattle is running through it. I hope I didn't disgrace myself yesterday, I really can't remember anything." He put his mouth under the cold-water faucet and let it run for several seconds. "Happy Christmas to you, too," he said, as he dried his face, "is there coffee?"

"Of course and I've got your present right here," she said, handing him a large, wrapped rectangle box, with a shiny red bow.

"Cassey, thank you," he cried, ripping at the paper. "Wow, it's wonderful, truly wonderful," declared Joe as he stared at the metal plaque that read, 'Mr. Joseph Carter – Photographer'.

"I thought you could put it on the door to your studio. I hope you don't mind me saying, Master Joseph, but I think it's time you tried to get over the grief of losing your pa and get on with your life. I know you want to be a professional photographer like Miss Diana, I'm sure it would make her proud."

"You're right, Cassey, it is time I got on with my life and stop wallowing in self-pity. I do want to make my mom proud … but now it's time, young lady, for your gift. I know I put it somewhere," he teased. "Oh yes, I remember, it's outside. Come on, close your eyes."

"Master Joseph, I hope you've not spent a lot of money on me." She laughed as he led her out to the carport. Opening her eyes, she let out a scream at the sight of a brand new blue convertible. "Master Joseph, is this really for me? No, I can't accept it, it's too beautiful."

"Of course you can accept it Cassey; after all you've done for me this year it's the least I could do and, anyway, who else have I got to spend my money on? You're like family to me. Here, take the keys, after breakfast perhaps we can take it for a spin."

***

Six days later, on New Year's Eve, Joe decided to make the effort and go out to a party. It was a huge relief for Cassey, seeing her master getting ready for an evening out.

"Well, how do I look Cassey? Will I do?"

"Master Joseph, every woman in the room will want to dance with you. Off you go now and have a good time. I need to get ready myself."

"Ok, Cassey, behave yourself, I'll see you next year."

The party, in a large open-plan house owned by a Mrs. Georgina Wilson – a youngish widow, well known in society circles – was in full swing when he arrived.

"Joseph, how nice of you to come. I haven't seen you out and about much since … well," she lowered her voice, "since the awful accident."

"It was nice of you to ask me, Mrs. Wilson."

"None of this Mrs. Wilson business, I'm Georgy to my friends. Come, let me introduce you to a few people."

As Georgy dragged a reluctant Joe around the room, he could not help but notice the sympathetic eyes following him as he passed by. Then, completely unexpectedly, a familiar face came into view.

"Joe, can I introduce you to Col. and Mrs. Harris."

Shit! Thought Joe, it's Carol's mother and stepfather.

"Hi, I'm Joe Carter."

Col. Harris removed an enormous cigar from his mouth and extended his arm towards him, shaking the younger man's hand with a stronger than normal grip to show his dominance. He was obviously a lot older than Carol's mother, a slightly stocky man with very short, military-style haircut. Joe immediately felt he was someone you didn't want to mess with.

"Nice to meet you, Joe, I'm John and this is my wife, Deborah."

"Oh please, call me Debbie. Haven't we met before Joe?"

"Yes, Mrs. Harris, I mean Debbie. I'm a friend of your daughter Carol."

"Right, well she's around here somewhere with her young man, I'm sure she'll be only too pleased to see you amidst all these old fogies, I know I am." She leaned in towards him, for a minute he thought she was going to kiss him, just as her husband pulled her away.

"Come on, my dear, how about a dance before you keel over and make an even bigger fool of yourself?"

Joe looked around him. Should he make a quick exit now before he encountered the girl of his dreams with his former best friend? Too late, he spotted them sitting in the corner oblivious to the rest of the people in the room. Damn, she looked just as beautiful as he remembered; how he ached for her.

"Angel, long time, no see."

"Joe. Look, I've been meaning to call you man ... I mean, what sort of friend am I? ... I should have been in touch. I just didn't know how things stood between us, I mean the last time we saw each other you wanted to punch my lights out."

Joe took a deep breath, "All forgotten ... all forgotten. Carol, looking good, life treating you well?"

Carol smiled at him. "Joe Carter, it's nice to see you again. Yes, as a matter of fact, life is treating me very well, I'm totally loved up with this hunk," she mocked, turning to Angel and kissing him full on.

Joe felt his insides churn. "Good, well, I'll leave you to it then." He started to walk away, but Angel disentangled himself from Carol and ran after him.

"Joe, do you fancy going out for a drink sometime? Sometime soon?" Angel asked eagerly.

"Ok, yes, I'd like that, give me a call, you know the number."

***

It was just before midnight when he turned into Fouracres. The headlights of his car shone out brightly in front of him, lighting his path. Just as his radio began the countdown to midnight, he drew up in front of the house and switched off the engine. Cassey was right; he had to pull himself together. He knew he would always lust after Carol, much more than he should, but it was time he made a life for himself and, when she was ready, he was somehow confident she would come to him.

CHAPTER 17 – A COMING TOGETHER

With the brass plaque reading 'Joe Carter – Photographer' proudly mounted on his studio door, Joe took a step back and smiled to himself. 1973 was flying by; he had already secured quite a lot of work – mainly, if he was honest, because of his name – and gradually, much to his satisfaction, his photographic portfolio was growing in size. He was finally back in society in a big way, meeting people again and he had even been on a few dates, mainly models. Nevertheless, behind his closed bedroom door, Carol was still the focus of his perverted fantasies – he was convinced that eventually they would be together. His plans for their wedding were stored in a safe place; ready to be resurrected when she finally agreed to be his. Yes, to the world outside, he appeared a normal upstanding young man, who any parent would be proud to have as a son-in-law. It was as if he were two different people in one body: a Jekyll and Hyde character who, at best, was a warm human being but at worst, when his anger overtook him, a cold-blooded killer.

His relationship with Angel was also on the up. His best friend had finally achieved his dream and had recently been enrolled in the Florida Police Force – Angel being a representative of the law surprisingly did not intimidate Joe in the slightest. They had been out and about together on several occasions since their reunion; most of the time just the two of them, for Carol usually had an excuse not to tag along. Over a year had now elapsed, with the murders of his father, Meme and Estelle so deeply buried in his mind, he actually was beginning to believe their slayings were a figment of his imagination, so confused with reality, on his dark days, was he becoming. It was March 1974 and he had arranged to meet Angel for lunch.

"So," Joe began, as he bit into his cheeseburger, "arrested anyone this week?"

Angel grinned. "Man, you ask me that every time I see you. No, but I was involved in a car chase yesterday: the idiot jumped a light, we caught him before he entered the highway so, a result."

"Great, I'll sleep easier in my bed now I know you're patrolling the streets," Joe teased. "By the way, it's your birthday next week, got anything planned?"

"Yes, my mom's talking about throwing me a family party on Friday, you can come if you want, that's if you're not jetting off to another photo shoot or anything?"

Joe took out his diary. "Great, yes, I should be back from New York by then, so all being well, I'll be there."

***

Cassey had just finished ironing Joe's new checked shirt for Angel's party when he entered the kitchen, half dressed, his muscular chest bare for the entire world to see.

"Thanks Cassey, you're a star, what would I do without you?"

"I'm sure you'd manage, Master Joseph," she said, averting her eyes from his naked torso as he took the warm shirt from her hands. It was on days like this she wished he looked upon her as a desirable woman, not simply the hired help. She was only a few years older than he was, born, of course, into totally different lifestyles. No, he would only ever see her as Cassey the maid and over the years she had learnt to accept that's how it would always be. She had to be content with the knowledge that he needed her in his life for her loyalty and friendship, no more than that.

***

Joe pulled up outside the Perez home just after seven-thirty. Angel's mother greeted him, as she always did, with an enthusiastic hug.

"Joe, you look a bit thin, are you eating well?" she asked, placing her plump warm hands on either side of his face, just as if he were a child. "There's lots of food and I've made a big bowl of that potato salad you like." She beamed as she stood aside, enabling him to enter the narrow hallway adorned from ceiling to floor with pictures of Angel's ancestors, past and present. Joe was always intrigued and, if he were honest, a little envious as to the vastness of the Perez family, his being almost non-existent.

"You certainly know the way to my heart, Mamma Perez," he said, bending down to kiss her full rounded face, a move that caused her already flustered cheeks to redden even more.

"Angel's just popped out with his pa and uncle to get some more beer; goodness knows how much alcohol they expect to be drunk tonight. My mom and two of my sisters are watching their game show in the front room, and Carol's already here," she began, lowering her voice to a whisper. "I think she and Angel might have had a bit of a falling-out, that's why I think he's gone with his pa, to let the situation cool a bit. Perhaps you could go and have a word with her. I've tried, but she almost bit my head off."

Joe found Carol on Angel's bed, curled up in the foetal position.

"Go away, I don't won't to talk to anyone!" she screamed on hearing the door creak open, but Joe was not leaving her in this state. This could be his moment, his time to get closer to the girl he loved.

"Trouble in paradise?"

"I said: go away, you don't know anything," she screeched, looking up with tearstained eyes. "Oh, it's you Joe. Well go on, close the door behind you."

Joe did close the door, however, he ignored her demand and remained in the room.

"If you need to talk, you'll find me a good listener," he said, sitting down on the edge of the bed.

"You're bloody persistent, aren't you, Joe Carter," she said, sitting up and drying her eyes with the back of her hand. "I bet I look a mess."

"You? No, never, you look just as beautiful as ever."

"Careful, I am dating your best friend, you know. Where is he, by the way?"

"Gone to get more beers apparently, to give you time to calm down."

"He's never been very good at dealing with people's feelings has Angel; always runs away when I need him the most."

"Well, I'm here."

"Yes, you are, aren't you?"

"So, why are you so upset?"

Carol's eyes began to well up again. "It's so difficult to talk about."

"Take your time, I'm not going anywhere."

She began to stroke the multi-coloured quilt covering Angel's bed with her fingers, reaching inside herself for the strength to begin.

"Ten years ago this weekend …" she began, almost chocking on her words, "I lost three members of my family and it was all my fault."

Joe moved further up the bed and took her hand. "Carol, you know I know how it feels to lose people you love. Tell me about it if you can, it just might help."

Carol rested her head on his chest and, automatically, he put his arm around her bare shoulders. He could feel his heart pounding harder; he hoped she could not hear the elevated sound – to his ears it was deafening.

"It was a Saturday … we were going on holiday; Mum, Dad, Nan and my brother Ryan … Ryan and I were always squabbling about something or another. Anyway, we were having one of our fights in the back seat of the car, Dad turned around for a split second to tell us off … he took his eye off the road, he didn't see the bus, it came from nowhere … Mum and I were the only survivors. I remember trying to shake my brother, but he wouldn't move, he wouldn't wake up. The firemen had to cut the roof off the car to get us out, I had barely a scratch and Mum had a broken leg and cuts to her face, but Dad, Ryan and Nan all died in the car – it was all my fault." She started sobbing, her tears saturating Joe's new shirt, drenching through it to his warm skin beneath.

"Listen Carol, whatever I say won't bring them

back. It was a terrible accident, pure and simple. If your dad hadn't taken his eyes off the road, if the bus hadn't been on the road at that precise time, there are so many if onlys. Accidents happen all the time ..."

Carol suddenly sat upright. "I'm so sorry, how could I have been so insensitive, you lost your dad and stepmother in that terrible fire. I bet you ask yourself everyday if only you had been there whether you could have saved them."

Joe hesitated briefly before replying, "Yes ... exactly... So you see, I know how you feel. I have no family left – you at least have your mom, try and think of that as a positive. I would give my life to have my mom back." Carol looked deep into his eyes and saw the sadness. "We have to support each other," Joe continued. "Let's make a pact here and now, to seek each other out when we are feeling unhappy. What do you say?"

"I must say, Joe Carter, that I underestimated you; you're not such a bad sort after all."

"I'll take that as a compliment, Carol Johnson." Carol smiled and kissed his stubbly cheek, just as Angel poked his head around the door.

"Not interrupting anything, am I? Is it safe to come in?"

"If you mean, have I calmed down? Then, yes, thanks to your friend here."

She planted her full lips on Joe again and he felt a surge of emotion run through him. Oh how he wanted to take her in his arms and kiss her back properly, but of course, for the moment, that was impossible.

***

It was in the early hours of the following morning when he finally arrived back home. Immediately, he

172

went down to his studio and opened the drawer holding all the wedding plans and laid them out neatly on the bench. He sat for a while just gazing down at the array of bits and pieces he had accumulated. He was convinced, now more than ever, that his fantasy would come true, for he had felt the warmth from her tonight, felt, dare he believe it, the love. Yes, she had definitely shown signs of love towards him. At least, that is what he had convinced himself. He could not wait to see her again, but for the time being, she would only truly be his in his dreams.

CHAPTER 18 – OH CAROL

It was Saturday night. Drifting off to sleep with her headphones pounding out the new chart hits, Carol's imminent slumber was brought to an abrupt halt when her mother, obviously intoxicated, stormed into her bedroom, an almost empty glass in one hand and a cigarette in the other. How she hated seeing her mother this way.

"He needs picking up from his thingy, I can't drive 'cos I've been drinking too, so you have to go and get him."

"Why can't he just get a cab?"

"Don't ask me! He wants you to pick him up, it's not far, should only take you twenty minutes."

"But Mum, you know I hate being alone in the car with him."

"I don't want another argument Carol – he wants you to pick him up, end of story. So be a good girl and do as I ask for once."

The streets were almost deserted when Carol began the drive to the golf club. She had not been kidding when she said she hated being alone in the car with her stepfather. Unbeknown to her mother, she had been putting money away for months now, to enable her to buy an airline ticket back to London. The thought of leaving her mum with that creep upset her, but she was more scared of what he might do to her on the days when they were left alone together. She had never told her mother or Angel about his sexual suggestions towards her, suggestions that were becoming more disgusting as time went on, mainly because he made her feel as if it was her own fault. He had drummed into her so many times that she was making him want her; she was leading him on and, if he did anything to her, no one would believe she had not asked for it. No, she had no choice; only a few more hundred dollars to go and she would be out of here.

Turning into the driveway taking her up to the main entrance to the golf club house, she caught sight of her stepfather sitting on the front step; the building behind him in darkness, apart from an outside light. Immediately, she brought the car to a standstill, he opened the passenger door and clambered in.

"You took your time." He leaned over towards her; his breath reeked of alcohol and his clothes of cigar smoke. "Not talking, huh? I told the guys tonight you'd be picking me up, shit were they jealous. I told them what a great lay you were and they believed me, the poor sods."

Carol kept her eyes forward as she put the car into drive and sped away from the building. They were almost halfway home when he started.

"You're eager to get back. I thought perhaps we could take a little detour, have some fun, what do you say?"

He placed his sweaty hand on her knee and squeezed it. Terrified of what he might try next, she put her foot down even harder on the accelerator, whereupon he seized the steering wheel and turned it sharply, causing the car to spin – instinctively she removed her foot from the pedal, at the very moment he reached down for the handbrake.

"Wow, Christ that was fun, I can feel the

adrenaline pumping. Now, how about a kiss? Then we can get in the back seat, more room there."

He made a grab for her; his enormous hands were everywhere, touching and pulling at her clothing. Somehow, with all her strength, she managed to push him off, clawing at his face as she did so, drawing blood before leaping out of the car. Running towards the freeway, she turned and in the dim light she could see his swaying figure attempting to follow her. Backtracking to her car, just as the full moon hid behind a cloud, she managed to restart the engine before her inebriated stepfather realised the situation. Roaring away from the scene, the eager wheels of the car caused a dust storm temporarily blinding her pursuer.

**

"Cassey, why don't you take yourself to bed, you look dreadful."

"If you're sure, Master Joseph. I must say this cough has gone right to my chest. I think I'll take some of that medicine I got from the drug store; at least it should help me to sleep."

"Yes, you do that, now off you go. I've got things to do. I'll be working downstairs most of the night, if you need me."

Grabbing the bottle of medicine from the cupboard, Cassey headed for her room. Climbing into bed, she poured out a large spoonful of Doctor Dan's cough remedy and, trying hard not to breathe in the unpleasant aroma it was discharging, put the spoon in her mouth and swallowed. Pulling the bedcovers up over her shoulders, she closed her eyes and prayed that by the morning she would feel a whole lot better.

After working hard for several hours on his latest project, Joe decided he needed a coffee break and left his studio to make his way back up to the kitchen, just in time to hear the buzzer from the gate.

"Yes?" he answered abruptly; annoyed that someone should be calling at this hour.

"Joe, it's Carol, can I come up to the house? Something's happened, I can't go home."

He was immediately troubled, hearing the desperation in her voice. "Carol, yes of course, my …" what he wanted to say was 'darling' but managed to stop himself, "I'll be at the door." He pressed the button to open the gates and waited. It was not long before he could see the headlights of her car. Drawing up in front of the house, she jumped out and fell into his open arms.

"Oh Joe, I was so frightened." He held her close and breathed in the sensual aroma of almonds, which always caressed her thick dark hair.

"You look as if you could do with a drink." He led her into the den and eased her into a chair.

Taking the glass of whiskey from his hand, she looked up at him. "I don't usually drink whiskey."

"Sip it slowly, it'll help to calm you. Now – only if you feel you can – tell me what's happened?"

Carol took several mouthfuls of the golden liquid before beginning her story.

"I had to go and collect my stepfather tonight from his golf club. Oh Joe, he attacked me near Glade Point. I was so frightened. I managed to scratch his face, though, before I got away. I can't go back home, I simply can't." Her tears were falling unrelentingly as Joe crouched before her and enveloped her in his

178

arms.

"The fucking bastard … you don't have to go home, Carol, there's plenty of room here. You can stay with me as long as you want to. I'll take care of you; you'll be safe here with me. No one will ever hurt you again." He delved into his pocket and drew out a tissue. "Here, dry your eyes."

"You're such a kind man," she said, reaching out with her right hand and gently touching his face.

"I'm glad you're realising that at last," he replied, his whole body aroused by her tender response.

She slumped back in her chair and continued drinking from the glass until it was completely empty.

"Feeling any better?" he soothed, removing the glass from her grasp.

"Yes, I think I am, thank you." Taking a deep breath, she took out her compact and applied her pink lipstick, before rising to her feet and glancing around her. "What a lovely room – you know this is the first time I've ever seen the inside of your house," she pointed out, "do you fancy giving me a tour?"

"What, right now? Are you sure you're up to it?" he asked, examining the line of her full, pouting lips; now enhanced, they cried out to be kissed.

"Yes, it will take my mind off what's happened, unless, of course, Joe Carter, it's inconvenient?"

How could he deny this goddess anything? "No, of course not. I was in the middle of making coffee when you arrived, I'll just go and get myself a cup. Would you like one?"

"No thanks, perhaps a drop more whiskey though; you were right when you said it would calm me."

He filled her glass once again before heading to the kitchen. He was in a dream: Carol, his Carol, was actually in his house, and what's more she was staying over. With a lightened step, he made his way back to the den. Pushing open the door, he instantly realised she wasn't there anymore. Her empty glass was on the table, but Carol was missing. Shit, she must have started the tour without him. Sprinting through the hallway, he began a frantic search in all the rooms, but there was no sign of her. Then, to his horror, he noticed the door to the basement ajar – damn, he realised he had not locked his studio.

"What the hell is this?" Carol demanded as soon as he entered. "What sort of sick shit are you? Why are there pictures of me all over the walls? You're no better than my stepfather!" It was at this point she caught sight of the wedding plans he had carelessly left out on the bench. "I don't believe it, are you insane? What's all this about?" she cried, picking up an invitation card. "Do you actually think in your warped mind that I would marry someone like you?"

Joe stood still while she pounded on his chest, screaming for answers. Was his dark dream about to come true? Should he take her now across the bench? His adrenaline was high enough, his desire to have her was almost overpowering. Grabbing her wrists, trying to restrain her, he kissed her hard, biting her lip in the process, before throwing her to the floor. She struggled beneath him, spitting in his face as she did so. For so long he had wanted her to want him, to love him like his mother had done. Why could she not love him? The hateful, vile words that were spilling from her mouth were tormenting his mind – anger was growing within him. His head was throbbing as his hands went around her neck, he started to squeeze and he continued to squeeze until her body stopped wriggling.

No! This was not how it was supposed to be. He was supposed to make love to her, not kill her. With her life now extinguished, Carol's body lay still on the cold hard floor.

The unexpected sound of a door banging somewhere in the house brought Joe back to his senses, nevertheless, he put that to the back of his mind as he began to grasp what he had just done. Cradling her in his arms, he held her close and began to wail – rocking backwards and forwards in his agony.

"Why did you make me do it? Carol, I'm so sorry, I didn't mean it, please don't leave me, you're all I've lived for all these years. I love you; there, I've said it. I love you Carol and I can't bear to think of my life without you." He laid down beside her body, stroking her hair, her face and then followed the contours of her breasts with his fingers. "I wanted to make love to you, I didn't mean to kill you. What's wrong with me?"

He leaned over and kissed her icy lips, before falling back beside her and closing his eyes. He knew he could not leave her here on the floor. He had no choice, of course, but to move her, however he could not bring himself to take her to the swamp and feed her to the alligators as he had done with Estelle – he might have ended her life but he would not be held accountable for the destruction of her beautiful body.

He rose and began to search around him; finding the overalls and gloves he had used before, he put them on. Lifting her up carefully, he ascended the steps to the hallway. She was not heavy, his Carol, he looked down at her and tried to imagine she simply asleep in his arms. Making his way outside, he placed her carefully in her car. Fortunately for him, in her rush to get out, she had left the keys in the ignition. The motor started easily. It was less than fifteen minutes' drive to Glade Point. Pulling in amongst the roadside foliage, he switched off the engine.

"Someone will find you soon, Carol. We would have been happy, you know, if only you'd just given us a chance." He opened the car door and, with a final backward glance, started to run back to Fouracres.

Arriving home just as the moon attained the highest point in the night sky, he poured himself a drink and kept pouring until the bottle was finished, then he reached for the phone.

"Mary, it that you? Oh wow. Mary, I'm so sorry. Mary, my wife ... she's left me. I made a terrible mistake, can you forgive me?"

Mary's voice at the other end sounded muffled. "Joe, there's nothing to forgive, it was a long time ago, I've moved on and so, it appears, have you."

"Mary, I need to see you. Please, fly over here? I'll pay the airfare, first class of course. Please, I really need a friend, please come for a holiday."

"Calm down Joe, I'm sorry, as I said I've moved on ..."

"At least think about it, Mary. Look, I'll give you my number. Please ... just think about it."

Replacing the receiver, the horror of what he had done enveloped his mind. He opened another bottle and took it up to his room.

***

Cassey hammering on his bedroom door awoke him from his alcohol-induced sleep.

"Master Joseph, your friend is downstairs, he's very upset. Can you come down please?"

Rising naked from his bed, he had to sit back down for a few minutes to get his thoughts together. His head was swimming. Did he have one of his dark dreams last night or did he actually kill Carol? He prayed he was wrong, oh how he prayed he was wrong. He pulled on shorts and a t-shirt and staggered downstairs; he had not quite reached the bottom step before Angel rushed at him.

"Joe, Carol's dead, her stepfather murdered her last night! Joe, Carol's dead!" He bellowed, throwing his arms around him.

Joe returned his friend's gesture, grasping him tightly, his guilt overwhelming him. So it was true. It was not one of his dark dreams; he had killed Carol. His mind was all over the place. He felt sick. Then he remembered the crystal tumbler sitting on the coffee table in the den, with Carol's pink lipstick still clinging to the side, evidence of her visit. Thinking quickly, he realised he had to steer Angel in the direction of the sitting room.

"I'm so sorry Angel, Christ, what a shock." He turned to Cassey, whose demeanour seemed traumatised by the news. "Cassey, will you bring coffee through to the sitting room please and make it strong?" The maid stood for a moment, looking searchingly at her master, before withdrawing.

***

"What happened?" Joe urged as he began to pace the floor.

Angel sat wringing his hands together, his eyes alert and staring. "A motorist came across her car with her body in it about four this morning," he began, almost choking on his words. "According to her mom, she had gone to pick up Col. Harris last night from his golf club ... she hadn't realised they hadn't come home because she had gone to bed and fallen asleep. A neighbour of the colonel found him laid out on her front lawn in the early hours. She told officers she had asked him about the scratches on his face and he had laughed and said his stepdaughter did it ... He bloody laughed, Joe!"

"So he confessed?" Joe stopped his pacing and looked down at his friend. He could feel the vein in his neck throbbing.

"No, not yet, he's still sobering up, but the team at the station know their job, it won't be long. Just put me in a room with him, I'll get the truth out of the bastard! I hope he gets the electric chair!" Angel jumped up and started punching the air. "I loved her Joe, I wanted to marry her ... I must get back, my mom's in bits. I must go."

"If I can do anything, anything at all, you know where I am."

Angel twisted around and directed his bloodshot eyes at him. "You loved her too, didn't you? Don't look shocked, I know you did. It's ok man ... I was never jealous. I know she had her problems, I know sometimes she thought I didn't care enough, but I did. I loved her, really loved her, and I'll do all I can to get her justice. You're a good friend. I'll let you know as soon as I have any news."

Joe watched as Angel drove away from the house in anguish at the devastation his dark side had caused.

Closing the front door, he immediately made his way down to his studio and started pulling all the pictures of Carol off the walls, throwing them and all the wedding paraphernalia into rubbish sacks before tying the bags securely. Leaving them for the moment, he made his way back upstairs to the den only to find Carol's glass had disappeared. He came across Cassey sitting at the kitchen table, holding her head in her hands.

"Are you ok, Cassey? It was terrible news, wasn't it?"

"Oh Master Joseph, that poor girl, she didn't deserve to die. Oh Master Joseph," she repeated, "I think I'm going quite mad."

"What do you mean you're going mad?"

She blew her nose hard on her rapidly disintegrating tissue. "The medicine I took last night, I think it made me hallucinate. Sometime after midnight, I got up to get myself a drink and I think I saw that girl, you know the one in the picture who looked like your mom, your friend Carol. I think I saw the girl that died, Master Joseph."

Joe sat down quickly as his legs gave way beneath him. "Cassey, it was a dream, as simple as that. Perhaps you shouldn't take any more of that medicine if it's making you see things that aren't there. Look, go back to bed, you need to rest, you'll never get over this flu if you don't rest."

Cassey stared blankly at him for a while before replying. "Yes, of course, you're right Master Joseph, I need more sleep. There's cold chicken in the fridge and plenty of salad and by the way, I've tidied up."

"Yes ... thank you." He realised, without her actually saying it, that she meant the glass.

185

"Everything will be fine Cassey, and so will you be, don't worry about anything. Now go on, get yourself back to bed."

***

Another bonfire crackled and spat, its angry flames reaching great heights in the intense heat of the afternoon, Joe stood back and watched as his future dreams melted away. He was sure Cassey would not repeat her nightmare to anyone; even if she believed it to be true, he knew he could trust her.

The phone in the house started ringing just as the fire began to die down.

"Joe, it's Mary, I want to take you up on that offer of a holiday, if that's ok?"

PART 4

CHAPTER 19 – ACROSS THE POND

The roar of the plane's engines, caused me to cling to the armrests of my seat, and as the airliner began its journey along the rain-soaked runway; picking up speed, just like a bird, it took to the air. I looked down at the green and brown fields that were passing rapidly beneath this giant of the sky, climbing higher and higher in its quest for altitude. I was totally in awe at the view below, nonetheless, I watched with despondency as the ground disappeared as we ascended into and then above the clouds. I sat back and closed my eyes. It was too late to change my mind now. I wondered if Dad had found my note? Was he angry with me, or did he understand my need to go? I had not said exactly where I was going, simply that I needed time on my own. Yes, he would understand and, anyway, I would phone him after I landed, to put his mind at rest – yes, surely he would understand?

"Excuse me, madam, can I interest you in a glass of champagne?"

I opened my eyes slowly and looked directly into the smiling face of an air hostess, with perfect white teeth, whose hat fascinated me, the way it seemed to sit so securely at an angle on the side of her head.

"Sorry, did you say champagne? I don't think I've got …"

"It's complimentary madam; you are in first class."

"Yes, yes of course, first class. Thank you." I sat

up in my seat and took the long-stemmed crystal glass from her graciously.

"We will be serving breakfast in a while, madam, if you would like to glance through the menu?"

"Thank you, you're very kind. Oh … are there toilets on board? Only I need to freshen up."

"Yes of course, madam, if you come with me I'll show you where they are. There is also a bar area with comfortable seating, if you feel in the need to stretch your legs."

So, this is how the other half live. Plush toilets and even showers, a bar area with a piano player, meals of smoked salmon and steak, endless amounts of champagne – yes, I could get used to this lifestyle.

Following a large breakfast, I returned to my seat and looked at my watch: 8.30 a.m. London time. I wondered if Dad had had any sleep or had he been on the phone all night trying to find me? Guilt was now weighing heavily on my shoulders, immersing my thoughts. It was not Dad's fault that Steve turned out to be a complete shit. Perhaps I should have waited and talked to him; explained how I had found my fiancé in bed with my so-called best friend. How could they? I started feeling nauseous again as the image of their betrayal re-entered my head; the vision of Violet completely naked sitting astride the man I loved. I bet he enjoyed every moment. I deliberated on how it came about. Obviously, she had followed him up to our hotel room. Did she knock on the door and, when he answered, did she simply throw herself at him, or had they arranged to meet and was he already lying naked in bed, waiting for her? I had to stop torturing myself with these thoughts, before they drove me completely mad.

Several hours and another meal later the pilot announced we were coming in to land. Fastening my seat belt, I looked out of the window. There were still clouds surrounding us, but somehow they were different to the ones we had left behind at home. Enormous billows of white candyfloss I had the urge to jump into, to become enveloped in their softness, their comfort. I swallowed hard as my ears began to pop from the air pressure. We were now through the clouds and I could see for the first time the coastline of a new continent below, a new country and perhaps even a new life.

It took ages to collect my luggage and then make my way through customs. I was exhausted having missed a proper night's sleep, however I soon forgot my weariness when I caught sight of Joe on the other side of the barrier.

"Mary, oh Mary, let me look at you."

He took me in his arms and for the first time in hours I felt completely safe and a sense of relief passed through me. Then I felt his lips on mine; warm friendly lips that were making my heart beat faster. Arm in arm, we made our way out of the airport and into a waiting car. We sat in the back seat, huddled up close together, gazing into each other's eyes.

What was I doing? Less than twenty-four hours ago, I was engaged to the man of my dreams and here I was with someone who I knew I could not trust, who took my virginity and then left me without any explanation to marry another woman. Was it revenge for Steve and Violet's infidelity that I was now cuddled up next to Joe? Did I imagine that he and I would marry, so I could stick two fingers up at my ex-fiancé and former best friend, as my new husband indulged me in our extremely wealthy life style? Yes, to my shame that is exactly what it was: revenge. Surely, I thought, I'm better than this.

The drive to Joe's home from Miami airport took several hours and with the gentle motion of the vehicle, I eventually closed my eyes and, resting my head on Joe's shoulder, I drifted off into a dream-filled sleep.

"Mary, Mary, we're here, welcome to Fouracres."

The sound of Joe's voice jolted me out of my slumber. My eyelids still felt heavy and focusing was difficult at first, but as I glanced out of the car's window, Joe's house came into view.

"Oh, Joe, it's wonderful. It's so big!"

The vehicle came to a halt at what I perceived as the main entrance and immediately Joe jumped out and lifted my bags from the boot of the car, before helping me out.

"Come on Mary, I can't wait to show you around."

He was so full of enthusiasm like a kid with a new toy – it was quite exhausting. The hall, like the rest of the house, was huge with numerous doors leading to rooms each with a unique style of their own.

"Mary, let's head to the kitchen, I want you to meet Cassey, my maid." Almost at a run, we arrived at the spacious, well-equipped room, which turned out to be unoccupied. "I'll just see if she's in her bedroom, she's not been well for a couple of days, she might be lying down. Feel free to help yourself to anything, perhaps a drink and something to eat?"

"I could do with a drink, a coke maybe?"

"Sure, there should be some in the refrigerator."

Joe disappeared for a minute or two, before re-emerging with a forlorn look on his face. "I was right, Cassey is not feeling at all well; she sends her apologies and hopes to see you later. So, Mary, can I get you anything else?"

"To be honest, all I want to do is sleep."

"The best thing for jet lag is to try and keep awake as long as you can," he coaxed. "I'll show you to your room later. In the meantime, let's go to the den, we've so much to talk about."

I followed him through to what he called the den, a very cosy room with a huge stone fireplace.

"This is all relatively new – the old den and my pa's study were destroyed in the fire. I know you didn't know what it looked like before, but I think the builders have done an excellent job restoring it to how it was."

"Oh my god yes, of course, the fire, how terrible for you to have lost both of your parents in such awful circumstances, everyone back home was devastated. We wanted to get in touch with you, but we didn't know how to contact you. How have you been coping?"

"I just had to get on with it, Mary. Anyway, it was my pa and stepmother who died in the fire, my own mom died several years ago from cancer. I still miss her terribly, she was everything to me." A great sadness erupted across his face and I put a comforting hand on his arm.

"I'm so sorry." I began to feel I was peeling an onion and, with each layer, I was finding out more and more about him. "You didn't know this but I lost my own mum last year from a heart attack. You and I have so much in common, we're like kindred spirits. Now, to add to your pain, your wife's left you."

He stared at me for a second or two, the colour draining from his face. "I'm sorry about your mom, she was a lovely lady. Mary ... I've got something to confess, I never did get married."

"I don't understand, what are you saying? I remember quite clearly, you phoned Edward on the day of your wedding and told him you were getting married and then the other day you told me your wife had left you."

He bowed his head, trying to avoid eye contact. "Mary, ever since the fire, I've ... I've had problems and when I drink ... I go into this ... fantasy world. I'm sorry to have lied to you and Edward. The other day, when I called you, I was upset and lonely, I was too drunk to know what I was saying. Your phone call yesterday, asking if you could visit after all, completely blew me away, I'm so happy you're here."

I just sat there, not able to move. So, it had all been a lie.

"But why, Joe? Why make up a wife? All you had to do was to tell me was you didn't want to marry me after all."

"At the time I was in a terrible place. My family had just been burned to death and I was alone, I think, to be honest, I went a little insane. Can you forgive, Mary?"

I was still trying to get it straight in my head. He had invented a wife and then made her disappear and, like a mug, I'd fallen for it. In my hour of need and desperation, I thought we both needed comforting; both needed a shoulder to cry on.

"I flew all the way here because something happened to me, Joe, which I can't bring myself to talk about just yet ... I thought ... Oh god, I don't know what I thought." Anger was rising rapidly within me. "Yes I do, I thought we had a lot in common; I thought we both needed each other, because we had both been let down by the one we loved the most. Now I'm beginning to believe I really don't know you at all. I mean, the last time we were together you asked me to marry you and then you took me to bed. When I heard you were getting married I felt distraught, used, and now I know you lied about the whole thing – well, I'm finding it hard to take it all in ... don't ask me to forgive you again, not yet!"

He tried to take me in his arms and kiss me, but I pushed him away.

"Please Mary, I need a friend."

"So do I Joe, I thought you were mine."

"I am, I really am. Look, it's not the best time to tell you, but I've got to go away for a few days. I tried to get out of it, but I've been working on a project, which has a deadline, and I've got to fly to New York later this afternoon. Cassey will show you the sights and look after you in the meantime. When I get back, we'll talk some more. You haven't told me yet why you decided to come over; I can see you're upset and not just with me. Come on, I'll show you up to your room, perhaps after a good sleep you'll see me in a better light."

He carried my bags up the staircase and I followed him, somewhat subdued. Yes, I was exhausted after everything that had happened and yes, I needed sleep, but I doubted I would be feeling any warmer towards him. I had been made a fool of again. I had travelled thousands of miles to find that out. From the top of the stairs, we walked along the landing. Coming to a halt, he turned and looked at me, before gripping the handle of the door, which opened into a beautiful room, decked all out in white.

"Mary, I hope you'll be comfortable in here. You have your own bathroom and television and there's plenty of closet space and the air-conditioning should keep you cool."

"Thanks Joe. Look, I'm sure you're right, I'm overtired and I just need to sleep. I'm really grateful to you for paying for my flight over here and letting me stay. I hope your trip is successful, I'll see you when you get back."

He leaned in towards me and kissed me, this time I let him. Once more I saw the sadness in his eyes, before he turned away, closing the door behind him. I have to admit, I felt somewhat relieved at his departure. I could not be bothered to unpack; I just wanted to slip under the sheets. The intense afternoon sun was beating down on the windowpane, so I pulled the curtains together, blocking out the blinding light before diving beneath the crisp cotton covers. I felt like crying, but I was even too tired to do that.

It was dark outside when I finally awoke, the clock on the bedside table said 2.30; I could not believe I had slept for almost twelve hours. I showered and washed my hair before making my way downstairs. I was desperate for a drink and something to eat. I opened the fridge and found a sandwich with a note from Cassey.

Sorry I missed you. I hope you slept well. There is Pound Cake in the tin on the table, enjoy. I'm usually up at around six, so I'll see you then. Cassey

I took the food and a large glass of milk back up to

my bedroom and switched on the radio next to the bed. With a full belly, I rested my eyes again and waited for 6 o'clock.

CHAPTER 20 – HOME TRUTHS

The strong light of the morning was beginning to break. I drew back my curtains and stared out of the window and breathed in the magnificent view of a white sandy beach and a vast ocean, which stretched out seemingly forever in front of me. Turning back into the room, I immediately realised, in my haste to fill my suitcase, I had not actually packed anything suitable for a hot climate; I would have to ask Cassey to take me shopping later. In the meantime, blue jeans and a long sleeved t-shirt would have to do. I stood in front of the bathroom mirror and pulled a comb through my hair. I was still in turmoil after Joe's revelation and was actually in two minds as to whether I should simply get straight back on a plane home. At least his temporary absence meant I had time to think more clearly about my next move.

I came across the elfin-like figure of Joe's maid, Cassey, busily preparing breakfast; she looked up as I entered her domain and I could not help but notice she looked a little startled at my appearance before her open face broke into a tight-lipped smile.

"Miss Macey … I'm Cassey. I'm so sorry I wasn't up to meeting you yesterday. I hope you slept well and that the sandwich I left was ok?"

"Yes, thank you, I appreciated that Cassey. It's nice to meet you. I do hope you're feeling better?" I extended my arm towards her and she did the same, albeit tentatively, obviously taken aback by my gesture of a handshake. "And please, call me Mary."

"Oh no, Miss Macey, it wouldn't be right. I know my place."

"I insist, Cassey."

She blushed and continued frying the streaky bacon in the pan, the aroma of which was very pleasing to my senses.

"Bacon with pancakes and syrup ok … Miss Mary?"

"Wonderful, thank you." Miss Mary was fine with me.

"I'll bring it through to the dining room."

"Can't I eat here in the kitchen? I don't want you to have to go to any trouble just for me."

"Well, normally, family and their guests eat in the dining room, but if that's ok with you, Miss Mary?"

She laid up the kitchen table and we sat down together, in silence at first; the vibe I was feeling from her was one of embarrassment – I guessed she usually ate alone.

"Master Joseph was sorry to have to leave you," she began eventually, "he asked me to take you anywhere you'd like to go, he's even left some money so you can treat yourself. He's always been very generous, has Master Joseph."

"Ok, thank you. If we could go shopping that would be great, I seem to have brought all the wrong clothes. I've never been anywhere hot before, you see, and I left home rather in a hurry." She viewed me curiously. "I had to get well away," I continued, "re-think my life and this is the first time I've ever been abroad."

"Did you meet Master Joseph in London then?"

"Not exactly, my brother Edward met him first when he came over here for a holiday and they began writing to each other. Then when Joe arrived in Europe, he came to us for a visit."

"I see. I've never been out of Florida before, let alone America. What's England like? It always looks foggy in films."

Her remark brought a grin to my face. "Well, when I left it was cold and wet, but we do have some wonderful warm, even hot, days in the spring and summer and of course, it's very green."

I felt nostalgic for a minute, thinking of my mum's garden back home, which, when I left, was beginning to fill with multitudes of spring flowers – the golden heads of daffodils, the mixed colours of tiny crocuses and the vivid blues of dwarf irises. I sighed, wondering if I would ever witness that scene again.

"Have you worked for the Carter family long, Cassey?"

"Almost eight years. Miss Diana, Master Joseph's mom, took me on after we met at the hospital. My own mom was going there for treatment. Miss Diana took me under her wing when ... my mom died."

"I see. Joe's mum sounds like she was a wonderful woman."

"Oh yes, she was the kindest person I've ever known. When she passed away, I was devastated and so was Master Joseph ... he's never really got over her death, you know."

I looked down at my now empty plate. "Yes, he certainly seems to have had his share of troubles. What were his father and stepmother like?"

Cassey rose to her feet and started clearing away the breakfast things. "My Master was a hard-working man, he was always kind to me," she broke off as she began to stack the sink with the dirty dishes, before continuing. "Then he married that woman, she was his secretary. I don't like speaking ill of the dead, Miss Mary, but she was evil, really evil." I could hear the unexpected venom in her voice.

"Did Joe get on with her?"

"No, Master Joseph hated her, she got Miss Diana's horse killed you know, it almost destroyed him when he came back and found out."

"When he came back? Do you mean from his trip to Europe?"

"Yes, from his trip to Europe, I've never seen him so upset before."

The sound of a telephone brought our conversation to an end and as Cassey left the room to answer it, it suddenly dawned on me that after everything that had gone on, I had not phoned my dad yet. Damn, he must be beside himself with worry. I followed Cassey out to the hallway in time to hear her completing her conversation.

"It was someone wanting to speak to Master Joseph," she said. "They didn't want to leave a message."

"If it was that important I'm sure they'll call again. Would it be alright for me to phone England?" I asked, "Only I left without telling anyone where I was going."

"Master Joseph told me to treat you as a member of the family and that everything was at your disposal. If you need the dialling code, you'll find it in the little book by the phone."

It took several attempts before I could hear the ringing tone vibrating through the airways. I had decided to phone the bakery, where I thought Dad would still be hard at work. A woman whose voice I did not recognise answered.

"Hello, Macey's Bakery, Lorraine speaking, can I help you?"

"Hello ... is my dad, Mr. Macey, there please? It's his daughter, Mary."

"Oh my, Mary, no, he's at the police station. Everyone's been worried about you. Can I give him a message?"

"Just tell him I'm fine, really I am, he's no need to worry. I'll call him again in a couple of days." With that, I rang off. Poor Dad, he must have been at the police station asking them to help him find me. Oh well, at least he'll soon hear I'm still alive, I could not do anything more from here right now.

"Miss Mary, if you would like to go shopping this morning, I could take you to the new mall that's just opened? It's not far away," Cassey pointed out.

"Thanks, that would be a bit of a relief. I'm beginning to feel quite warm in these clothes, I'll go and get my handbag."

We had a lovely morning shopping in the mall; I did not even feel guilty about spending Joe's money – after all he'd put me through, I believed he owed me. I thought of Edward when he had come over to Florida for a holiday, how I had teased him about the clothes he had brought back. I hoped my brother was ok and not worrying too much. Oh god, it was slowly dawning on me about the rashness of my behaviour. Mary Macey, the normally boringly sensible one; well, I was not so boring and sensible anymore, was I?

**

It was mid-afternoon and I was feeling tired,

nevertheless I managed to fight the urge to sleep by busying myself. Cassey had made us a lovely lunch and now, feeling cooler in my new cotton dress, I was in the study looking through the library of books when I heard the sound of a buzzer at the front door. I could hear Cassey talking to whoever was at the other end of the intercom, before she came to speak to me.

"Sorry to disturb you, Miss Mary, but it's Master Joseph's friend at the gate. I've let him in, he knows Master Joseph's not here but he sounded stressed, which is not surprising, under the circumstances."

"I don't understand Cassey, what circumstances?"

"The murder of his girlfriend, it only happened a couple of days ago. Didn't Master Joseph tell you?"

"No, not a word. How terrible. What's his friend's name?"

"Angel Perez, he's a police officer … there he is now."

Cassey opened the front door to a dark-haired, handsome young man dressed in shorts and a very bright shirt.

"Sorry Cassey, I know you said Joe isn't here, but I've been driving around, my head's all over the place … man, I just needed to talk to someone other than my family."

Cassey looked at him, then at me, as I appeared by her side. "This is Master Joseph's friend from London, England: Miss Mary Macey. Miss Mary, this is Police Officer Perez."

"Please, it's Angel, I'm off duty. It's nice to meet you, Mary." His voice was perfectly controlled, nonetheless his face gave his torment away.

"Likewise, please, come on in." I led him straight

through to the sitting room.

We sat chatting for several minutes; I told him how Joe and I had met, and he explained that they were old friends going way back. Then, inevitably, the conversation came around to the recent murder of his girlfriend. The poor man immediately began to fall to pieces, just as Cassey entered with a tray of drinks.

"I'm sorry," he began, his face reddening in his anguish. "I loved her so much Mary, I was going to marry her. I think Joe loved her too, in his own way."

I suddenly recalled the conversation Joe and I had had in London, about a girl he fancied in his hometown. Was it the same girl, I wondered?

"What was the name of your girlfriend?"

He hesitated for a minute or two, seemingly finding it too painful even to speak it.

"Carol, her name was Carol ... she was English, like you, in fact ..." he began, gazing at me through narrowing eyes, "you look very much like her." These remarks, for some reason, made me feel a bit uncomfortable.

The unexpected sound of Cassey dropping the metal tray on the wooden floor startled both of us. I looked up at her face and, for a moment, I thought I saw genuine fear.

"Cassey, come and join us?"

"No, Miss Mary, I couldn't."

"Please sit, you've been on your feet all day." Cassey looked quite nervous as she perched tentatively on the edge of a chair, whereupon I turned back to Angel. "Do the police suspect anyone?"

"That's the thing, they did have her stepfather, Col. Harris in custody – man, I thought it was all cut and dried. Then, this morning a patrolman reported he had been parked at Glade Point about the same time Col. Harris was found in a neighbour's garden and there had been no sign of Carol's car. So the police realised it couldn't have been him after all and they've let him go. They think someone else killed her and dumped the car, and her body, in the early hours of the morning. Now I don't know who killed my beautiful girl!" He bent forward and clasped his hands to his head.

"You poor man, I don't really know what to say, except if her stepfather is innocent, isn't it best the police know it now so they can concentrate on finding the real killer, before the trail goes cold?"

Angel sprang to his feet. "Yes, of course, you're right and I should be out there helping them, I'm just not thinking straight." He marched out of the sitting room towards the front door while Cassey and I trotted behind him. "It was really great meeting you Mary, perhaps when Joe gets back we can get together for a drink or something."

"Yes, that would be nice. Good luck, I hope they find whoever killed her really soon."

His car created a wall of dust as it sped away in his haste from the house. I turned to Cassey.

"Right, we need to have a chat Cassey. I saw the expression on your face just now, you looked frightened, do you want to tell me why?"

She began to walk briskly away from me towards the kitchen and I followed closely at her heels. Suddenly, she turned and with a look that immediately shocked me, spoke with unfamiliar clarity.

"Miss Mary, I think you should go back to England before Master Joseph gets back."

I was rather taken aback by this sudden assertiveness on her part.

"I see. Do you want to explain why?"

"I think ... your life could be in danger."

"In danger? Do you mean from Joe? Why would I be in danger from Joe?"

She went to a cupboard and took out a small bottle of brandy and proceeded to pour it out into two glasses before handing one to me.

"Drink, Miss Mary, I think we'll both need it after what I'm about to tell you."

I sat down at the table, fear mounting in me as to the disclosures she was about to impart.

"The night that that poor girl was murdered, I saw her here in the house. Master Joseph tried to convince me I was hallucinating, which I thought I was at first because of the medicine I was taking for my cough, but I wasn't; I know I saw her. I even found a glass in the den smeared with lipstick."

"Oh my god, are you telling me you think Joe murdered her, here, in the house?"

"Yes, I think it's a strong possibility."

"Why didn't you say anything when Angel was here?"

"Because I can't be a hundred percent sure that he actually killed her. I don't want to get Master Joseph into trouble without any real evidence. I'm very fond of him, you see, and if I'm wrong, it could ruin his life. If he did do it, I'm sure it was an accident ... yes, that's what it must have been, an accident." She took a large swig of brandy from her glass. "I think Officer Perez was right, when he said that Master Joseph was in love with her. He had pictures of her, lots of pictures and ... well, I believe she reminded him of

Miss Diana. When Officer Perez said you looked like his Carol, I think, Miss Mary, Master Joseph chose to befriend you for that reason, because you look like Carol and Miss Diana, I couldn't help but notice the resemblance the minute I met you."

I was in turmoil; of course, I knew only too well what Joe was capable of, but surely he was not capable of murder?

"I do hope you're wrong, Cassey. Look, we have to do something ... How about we search his room, see if we can find any evidence?"

"Oh no, Miss Mary, I don't think we should."

"Really? You're fine with not knowing whether or not we're living with a killer?"

***

His bedroom was very neat and tidy; nothing at first glance seemed to be out of place. I did believe Cassey's supposition was right; if Joe had ended Carol's life then it must have been an accident – in my heart, I was sure I would know if he was a killer. We started rummaging carefully through drawers and closets, working in silence, two strangers thrown together in desperation to find out whether the young man, so dominant in their lives, had something unbearable to hide. However, we found nothing to incriminate him in Carol's murder, which actually was a relief. Of course, if we were honest, we had no idea what we were expecting to find anyway. We were just about to leave when, at the last minute, I decided to look under his bed and that's where I found it: the locked wooden box. Instinctively, I knew I had to open it.

"Help me Cassey, I need a nail file or something?"

It took us several minutes, but eventually we managed to force the lock. I lifted the lid and stared down at the leather bound book held within its walls, whereupon Cassey immediately gasped at our find.

"It's the journal I gave Master Joseph when he left for Europe."

Removing the book from its hiding place a small photograph fell to the floor. Turning it over, I realised at once it was the picture of me that Edward had brought over with him when he came here on holiday. So, my brother had not lost it; Joe had stolen it, just like he had stolen my purse.

Gradually, we began to turn the pages of the private journal, both horrified at the words we were slowly digesting. Joe's innermost thoughts, written down in black and white, along with depraved and disgusting confessions which not only incriminated him, but also brought us much distress. Nevertheless, we did not give up and kept on reading, wanting to know; trying to understand why he would have done such things. With the last entry, written two days ago, Cassey and I finally reached out for each other, holding hands and trembling as we did so.

All I wanted was for Carol to love me, why wouldn't she love me? Am I so unlovable?

CHAPTER 21 – NO HIDING PLACE

Cassey and I sat in silence, absorbing the writings of a young man that had blown our worlds apart. Joe Carter was a serial killer. He had ended the lives of four human beings and we were the only ones, apart from him, who knew about his inexcusable murders. What had we unleashed by finding this document? More importantly, what the hell should we do with it now? I threw the book in revulsion onto his bed.

"I wish we had left it alone!" Cassey screamed hysterically. "I knew it was a bad idea to search his room. Are you happy now? Master Joseph's a killer, a goddamn killer!"

She threw herself to the floor, sobbing uncontrollably.

"Get up Cassey, and pull yourself together," I cried, dragging her to her feet. Surprisingly, under the circumstances, I felt reasonably calm at this point. "Well, as far as I can see, we have two choices, we either put the book back where we found it or we hand it into the police. Whatever we do, we can't stay around here; we must leave now, tonight."

Cassey stared at me, her eyes inflamed from crying. "I can't leave him, I can't leave Master Joseph."

"Cassey!" I began, sitting her down on the bed, holding her arms firmly, shaking her, wanting her to listen to reason. "Please, you and I have just read the confessions of a killer; when he realises we know, he will probably want to end our lives too. I for one don't want to hang around to give him the opportunity. We need to go. We'll both pack a bag and you can drive us to a hotel in town so we can think this out properly, but we do need to leave!"

Cassey picked up the book again and held it tightly to her chest. "I don't think he was born a killer, Miss Mary, do you? He was such a wonderful young man, devoted to his mom. They did everything together you know. I think when Miss Diana died, he started searching ... for someone to replace her so he could love again."

I lowered myself down on the bed next to her. "No Cassey, I don't think he was born a killer, but I do think he's a very disturbed young man who needs help before he kills again and we are the only ones who can make that happen."

She passed the book over to me. "I know you're right, it's just such a shock. Can I tell you a secret I've never told anyone else before?"

"Of course you can."

"I love him – I know he's never looked twice at me, but I can't help the way I feel; believe me, I've tried." The poor girl, in love with a man who only sees her as a friend and now she finds out he's a killer and she still loves him. "Did you ever love him, Miss Mary?"

"For a little while, I thought I did, but that was another lifetime ago."

I put my arm around her and we sat for a moment in contemplation.

Finally I got to my feet, still clutching the journal. "Right, we'd better go. When were you expecting Joe back?"

"He told me he should be back some time tomorrow morning, so that should give us plenty of time. What are we going to do with the journal?"

"Well ... if we put it back where we found it, he'll soon notice the lock has been tampered with and probably destroy it. So, we'll have to take it with us; after all, it's the only real evidence of his crimes we have."

Still obviously mulling over the past, Cassey rose and started for the door. "If Miss Diana hadn't died, or if his stepmother hadn't destroyed Cheyenne, then perhaps none of this would have happened and Master Joseph wouldn't have become a murderer."

"Sometimes it just takes a trigger in your life to start down the wrong road, Cassey. I've no doubt Meme was an awful woman, but there are other ways to get evil out of your life without resorting to murder. I mean, we've both lost our mothers, had our lives turned upside down, and we haven't resorted to crime, at least, I know I haven't."

We made our way to our respective rooms and started packing. I was now in hell as the enormity of the situation began sinking in. Not only had I slept with a murderer, but Cassey had read that fact with her own eyes. Handing the journal over to the police meant they and god knows who else would also read about my shameful past. I knew deep down we had no other choice, of course, other than to expose Joe, however, with Cassey admitting to me she loves him – when push came to shove, could I rely on her to do the right thing?

We met in the hallway twenty minutes later.

"I'll go and bring my car around, Miss Mary."

"Cassey, I think it would be ok for you can call me just Mary now, don't you think?"

She managed a watery smile before disappearing

from my sight. She had only been gone a few seconds when she suddenly reappeared with a look of horror on her face.

"I've just seen the headlights of a car at the gates, it must be Master Joseph returning early, otherwise the driver would have buzzed through to the house by now."

I gazed out along the driveway; sure enough, a car's piercing headlights were making their way rapidly towards us. We grabbed our bags and started to run to Cassey's car. Scrambling in, we crouched down and watched and waited in trepidation as the driver brought the car to a halt in front of the house. When we caught sight of the occupant, it only confirmed our fears. Swiftly mounting the steps to the front door, Joe fumbled with his keys before disappearing from our sight. Instantly, Cassey started the car's engine and, putting her foot down on the accelerator, we headed out towards the front gates in terror at the situation we had found ourselves in. Removing the gate's remote control from her pocket, Cassey clicked once. Nothing happened, so she clicked again, still nothing happened.

"Master Joseph must have disarmed the gate from the house!" Cassey cried, "He knows, Mary! He knows we've read the journal!"

"Don't be so stupid, of course he doesn't know, he wouldn't have had time to go up to his bedroom. No, either he heard us leave and panicked or the damn gates are simply not working. We must keep calm, think, why would we be leaving in such a hurry? I know, we'll tell him I'm having an asthma attack and you were taking me to hospital."

Unfortunately for us, there was no other exit from

Fouracres except for the beach – and I for one did not fancy swimming with sharks, so we had no choice but to return to the house and try and bluff our way out of the situation we had found ourselves. We could see Joe standing with crossed arms in the doorway as we approached – I managed to shove the journal underneath my seat before the car came to a standstill.

"Cassey, I'll distract him while you phone the police," I whispered. Still staring out in front of her, she nodded.

Joe descended the steps from the house at full speed. He paused beside the car, scrutinizing me at first through the passenger window, before finally opening the door.

"Where were you ladies off to?" he asked, deep frown lines appearing on his face.

"Oh Joe ... the gates seem to be faulty ..." I began, "Cassey was taking me to hospital, it's my asthma, I was having an attack and my pills didn't seem to be working."

"Funny, I had no problems with the gates. I'll phone someone tomorrow to come out and fix them. Anyway, how are you feeling now?"

"Actually a little better, thank goodness. I'm sorry we didn't wait to tell you we were leaving, I freaked out, Cassey was just trying to help me."

"That's Cassey all over, always there to lend a hand in difficult circumstances, aren't you Cassey?" Was it my imagination or did his voice sound cold?

He glanced across to Cassey, who was still staring out in front of her, her hands seemingly glued to the steering wheel.

"Right, well, you both had better come back in, we

have a lot to talk about Mary, I want to tell you about my trip and I want to hear what you girls have been up to."

He helped me out of the car; fortunately, in the darkness he didn't seem to notice our bags hiding in the shadows of the back seat. Finally managing to release herself from the steering wheel, Cassey emerged from the driver's side.

"We … didn't expect you back until tomorrow, Master Joseph, it's a nice surprise …" Cassey stuttered.

"The meeting finished earlier than expected. I thought, why should I stay any longer when there are two lovely ladies waiting for me at Fouracres? So I came home and I'm really glad I did. You obviously both need looking after. You still look quite pale Cassey; I really don't think you've quite got over that flu, you know. Come on, let's get into the house."

He led us by our arms, straight into the hallway. "Let's go into the kitchen and I'll make us all something to eat."

"Oh no, Master Joseph, I can manage dinner. I've already prepared those hamburgers you like, they won't take me long to cook. You and Miss Mary should go into the den and I'll call you when they're ready."

"Well, if you're sure. Come then Mary, come and put your feet up."

I felt an icy chill run through me as soon as we entered the room, knowing now that this was where his first murders took place. Granted, everything around us was new, however the ground it occupied was the same. Were the spirits of his father and Meme haunting these walls, crying out for justice? I tried hard to understand the anger that drove him to kill, that led him to become the monster he turned out to be. For that was what he was in my eyes: a monster.

"Mary, you're very quiet, I might even say distant."

"Sorry Joe, I'm afraid I'm not going to be very good company this evening." He sat down next to me and took my hand.

"Mary, you're shaking, can I get you anything?"

"It's the tablets, they always make me shake. It's helping, you sitting here with me though."

Oh god, I hoped Cassey was trying to call the police, I did not know how long I could keep up this pretence. Where were the phones in the house anyway? I knew there was one in the hall, one in the study and one in his bedroom. Would Joe hear Cassey using either of them from here? It was too quiet; I had to create some noise.

"How about turning on the television? I haven't watched anything since I've been here."

"I thought we were going to talk, Mary?"

"I know, but I'm still feeling a bit weak, we can always talk later, can't we, Joe? Unless you want rid of me, of course?"

The minute the words left my mouth, I swallowed hard and went quite red – but fortunately he seemed to be ignorant of the innuendo, which I was more than a bit relieved about and, with a sigh, he got up and switched on the television.

***

Cassey took the hamburgers from the fridge and threw them onto the cold griddle. She knew Mary was right, of course; she had no choice but to call the police. Nevertheless, as frightened as she was, it was going to be the most difficult thing she had ever done. She slipped off her shoes and began to make her way across the hallway to the study. The sound of the television suddenly blaring out masked her progress over the wooden floor. Entering the study, she reached the desk and lifted the black phone to her ear and commenced dialling.

Tears were now cascading down her cheeks and, with her voice faltering slightly, she spoke softly into the mouthpiece. "Hello … police, I'm calling from the Carter residence, I want to report a murder …"

A large hand suddenly appeared and immediately disconnected the call. Joe stood defiant before her and, grabbing her by her wrist, he wrenched the receiver from her grasp.

"Cassey, it's just as well I've got excellent hearing, what the hell are you doing in here? Were you talking to the police?" he demanded. Dissolving into a quivering mess, Cassey stood in front of him unable to speak "You were talking to the police, weren't you?" he yelled. "Why would you do that? I told you, it was the medicine making you hallucinate the other night. Carol was not here!" he bellowed, bending the poor girl's arm, causing her to cry out in pain. "For Christ's sake, girl, after all I've done for you. You know you've made me very angry and I'm not nice when I'm angry, even to those I love."

"Oh Master Joseph, I …"

"Let her go, Joe!" I screamed, storming into the room. "I told Cassey to call the police because we know you murdered Carol!"

With an expression of a wild beast, he released his hold on Cassey and lunged at me, knocking me to the floor. His hands were around my throat as he started to squeeze. I began to lose consciousness just as the sound of a gunshot reverberated around the room, at which point the pearl-handled firearm slid effortlessly across the floor.

PART 5

CHAPTER 22 – AN INVESTIGATIVE MATTER

Brook Cottage was deadly quiet as Josie closed the folder; she sat for a moment, digesting the words that had caused her whole body to tremble. Leaving the comfort of her wing-backed chair, she moved into the kitchen and switched on the kettle. It was Sunday; Linda would be around soon to collect her for their lunch date. She glanced out of the window, just in time to see Sandy playing with a mouse outside on the patio. He was tossing the tiny creature high in the air, pushing it with his paw after it hit the ground, wanting the poor thing to move, to give his inner evil something to chase. Damn that cat; he knew full well she was terrified of mice, why oh why, did he continue to bring them anywhere near the house, especially when Max was away?

"It's only me," cried Linda as her most welcome face appeared around the kitchen door. "I rang the front door, sweetie, but you obviously didn't hear me. Are you ready to go or are we having a cup of tea first?"

"Tea first, I think. Isn't Sabrina with you?"

"No, she says we're too boring to spend any time with, so I've dropped her off at a friend's house – teenagers, huh?"

Sabrina was Linda and Richard Blake's daughter, born a year after they got married. She was a lovely girl, but she had reached that awkward age when she thought her parents were too embarrassing to be seen anywhere with.

"Is this the manuscript you've been talking about?" asked Linda as the friends sat down together in the front room.

"Yes, I finished it just before you came."

Opening the folder on the coffee table, Linda started skimming through the pages. "Well, any good?"

"Yes, Pat's got quite an imagination, although I don't think she's finished it yet. Why don't you take it and read it? I'm sure she won't mind."

"Ok then, I'm quite a fast reader and a drinker of tea. With that little bit of information, my dear friend, are you ready to go?"

***

Monday morning and Max was due back from his boy's only weekend, so Josie was up early doing a quick tidy up before going off to work, when there was a knock at the door. Doctor O'Brien stood in her porch, Josie thought, looking unusually anxious.

"I'm sorry to disturb you Mrs Forrester, but I've been ringing Mrs. Wood's door and she's not answering. Do you know if she's away?"

"Not as far as I know, doctor. Do you want me to come next door with you? I do have a key to her house if you think we need to get inside."

"Yes, I wouldn't be worried except that she had an appointment at the hospital this morning, which she really needs to keep. I told her I would collect her and take her before surgery, to make sure she got there on time."

Josie soon found the key and together she and the doctor walked up the path to Honeysuckle Cottage and rang the doorbell again; still no answer – two pints of milk were curdling on the doorstep. Josie led the way through the side gate and around to the back door.

"Her curtains are still closed, which is unusual for Pat, doctor, she's normally up bright and early."

Doctor O'Brien sighed. "I think, Mrs. Forrester, you should use your key."

Although this was not the first time Josie had let herself into Pat's cottage, it was the first time she was using her key without Pat's prior knowledge. This time, Josie felt uncomfortable, as if she was an intruder invading her neighbour's privacy. The back door opened directly into the tiny, country-style kitchen. Wiping their feet on the doormat, Doctor O'Brien called out Pat's name. There was no reply. They walked cautiously into the dark narrow hall, both calling her name simultaneously. The whole place smelt sort of musty. Opening the door to her sitting room, they peered in, but there was still no sight or sound of Pat, even the clock over the mantelpiece was silent. Doctor O'Brien put his right foot on the bottom rung of the stairs and gripped the banister, before turning and gazing at Josie, a grave look breaking out across his face.

"You can wait downstairs if you want to, Mrs. Forrester."

"Doctor, do you think ... something awful has happened to her?" Josie whispered.

"I don't know, but if you want to stay down here, I will understand."

Josie shook her head and followed on behind as he

led the way upwards, hesitating each time the stairs beneath their feet creaked loudly, seemingly crying a warning of impending doom. They both felt it, the icy coldness. The air around them was still, as Doctor O'Brien turned the ancient handle to Pat's bedroom.

Reeling from the aroma of vomit that invaded her nostrils, Josie's entire being shuddered at the sight that meet her eyes. In the dim light of the room, beneath the bedcovers, a look of agony frozen on her aged face, lay Pat.

"Oh my god, doctor …" Josie gasped her tear ducts filling and overflowing down her cheeks. "She's dead!"

Doctor O'Brien moved swiftly towards Pat's bedside and gently touched her forehead.

"Yes, sadly, she looks as if she's been dead for several days." He pulled up the duvet to cover her face, before reaching into his pocket for his mobile. "I need to make a few phone calls – you look as if you could do with a sit down, Mrs. Forrester. I'll wait here for the ambulance, perhaps I could pop round later for a cup of sweet tea, I think we could both do with one."

"Yes, of course, I was supposed to be going to work, I'll have to make a few phone calls myself. This has all been a bit of a shock."

Back in her own cottage, Josie waited patiently for the doctor's return. She heard the ambulance and then watched from behind her curtain as Pat's body was carried out in a zipped-up black bag along the path of Honeysuckle Cottage for the very last time. Sitting down in front of her fireplace, Josie sobbed quietly for her friend and neighbour.

Doctor O'Brien was as good as his word and

called round before he left for his surgery.

"Are you ok, Mrs. Forrester? You're still looking a little pale, have you called someone to be with you? Can I prescribe you anything?"

"I'm fine, really I am. It was just so all unexpected. I've spoken to my husband, Max; he'll be home soon. Have you any idea how Pat died, doctor?"

"I'm not sure, there will be a post-mortem, as there often is when someone dies unexpectedly at home, so hopefully that should tell us." He lifted the mug of hot tea to his lips.

"You don't think she died from natural causes then?" Josie asked.

"I didn't say that," he said. "I ... well, I didn't expect her to die just yet. By the way, it's best if you don't enter her house again, until we know for sure her cause of death."

Josie was slightly shocked at this statement; what was he inferring? Finishing his tea, he got up to leave.

"Her face, doctor, was that normal? I mean, she looked like she was in agony before she died," cried Josie.

Doctor O'Brien looked at Josie through weary eyes. "Mrs. Forrester, it was unfortunate that you had to see your friend like that, but I'm not prepared to say any more until I get the autopsy report. I really am sorry."

***

It was later that same day, and just as Max pulled the local paper out of the letterbox, he heard an unexpected commotion outside. Gazing out from their front window, he was surprised to see a police car parked in the lane and several police officers sealing off Honeysuckle Cottage with tape. Calling up to Josie, she quickly joined him and as they watched from the comfort of their lounge, they observed a man and a woman in civilian clothing walking up their path.

"Mr. and Mrs. Forrester, I don't know if you remember me? I was involved in the Borelli case?" pointed out the attractive, amber-eyed brunette, as Max opened the front door.

"Oh yes, of course, WPC Brown, how nice to see you again," replied Josie. "Please come in."

"It's actually Chief Inspector Adams now," she responded, showing them both her warrant card, "and this is Detective Sergeant Stone."

"Right, promotion and marriage, congratulations. What can we do for you, inspector?"

Max was quick to notice that Detective Sergeant Stone seemed a little too curious about his surroundings. Steering the detective's prying eyes away from their personal effects, Max motioned to Josie to bring the inquisitive detective to her attention, before offering them both a seat.

"We're here because we're making inquiries into the death of your neighbour, Mrs. Pat Wood. I understand, Mrs. Forrester, you were one of the last people to see her alive?"

"Just a minute inspector, are you saying that her death was suspicious? Only my wife has had a very traumatic day, can't your questions keep until tomorrow?" Max interrupted, alarmed at the possible implication directed at Josie.

"Max, I can answer for myself and anyway, darling, you weren't here; I'd rather get the questions over and done with. I'm sorry inspector, I'm a bit confused; are you saying her death wasn't from natural causes? I know the doctor had asked for a post-mortem, have they found something already?"

"No, it's too early for those results, but the doctor has voiced his concerns about her death, in fact, I'm sorry to go as far as saying we're looking into a possible murder."

Max and Josie reeled at these words. "A possible murder? You're not sure whether she was murdered or not?" demanded Max.

"No, as bizarre as it seems. The forensic team are in there now. Hopefully we'll know more when they've finished and, together with the results from the post-mortem, we should soon have a better idea of what happened to Mrs. Wood. Going back to the last time you saw her. Sorry, do you mind if I call you Josie and Max, as I used to, only it seems strange for me to keep calling you Mr. and Mrs. Forrester, I know it's not very professional."

Josie smiled. "Of course, it's fine and, just so we're on even ground, what's your Christian name? I've only ever known you as WPC Brown."

Chief Inspector Adams looked over at her colleague, apparently seeking approval before replying, "It's Samantha, but you can call me Sam."

"Right, Sam, the last time I saw Pat alive was last Friday morning; she came round to bring me a manuscript."

Sam looked quizzically at Josie. "A manuscript? Was she an author?"

"Well, no, not as far as I'm aware, this was the only thing she had ever written."

"Do you still have the manuscript?"

"No, I passed it on to my friend Linda and, with everything that's been going on, I forgot to ask her for it back. I guess it doesn't matter now Pat's dead."

"I guess not. Going back to that Friday," Sam began, as Detective Sergeant Stone scribbled frantically in his notebook, "how did Mrs. Wood seem to you that day?"

"Fine, from what I can remember. I know she had been to the doctor's, but she said he had told her there wasn't anything to worry about; that she was in good health considering her age."

"Right, I see."

"Look Sam ..." began Max, who was becoming irritated at the direction the questions were taking. "Are you implying that Josie had something to do with her death?"

"I'm afraid everyone is under suspicion at this point in time, Max; as I said it's a possible murder, and I'm not ruling anything or anyone out." She turned back to Josie, "I have no more questions for you at the moment, thanks for your time. We might of course need to talk to you again, so don't leave the country," she joked, looking directly at Max who cracked a smile back before closing the door behind them.

***

The walls of Brook Cottage were filled with the laughter of children, a wondrous sound to Josie's ears after the week's events. It was two days later and Josie's daughter Beth and her best friend Kate had come round with their children for tea.

"Mum, have you heard anything more from the

police?" asked Beth, stuffing a cream doughnut into her mouth.

"No, the whole thing's gone a bit quiet. I did notice there was a policeman next door this morning removing the tape, so I'm guessing they've finished their examination of the property. I haven't heard anything about a funeral."

"I still can't believe Aunty Pat's dead; she was such a character, always wanting to know everyone's business, I guess because she had no family of her own."

"How long had she lived next door?" Kate enquired.

"Max and I were only talking about that the other night. I think it must be at least twenty years; a young couple lived there before her."

They finished their meal and played hide and seek for a while with the children until the adults – not the children - were, quite frankly, exhausted.

"Thanks for the tea, Mum, sorry to have missed Dad – tell him I'll see him at the weekend," said Beth, as she kissed her mother goodbye.

"Yes, he'll be sorry to have missed you and Christopher, and you and the twins of course, Kate," added Josie as she helped her grandson struggle on with his coat.

"I'm sorry about the vase, Josie," said Kate apologetically, bringing to mind the shattered glass vessel, the consequence of the twins throwing a ball in the house. "I'll try and find a replacement when I'm in town next."

"Oh, not to worry, accidents happen – it had a chip in it anyway; I should have thrown it away weeks ago."

Walking them down to their car, Josie looked up as a red Honda drew up outside Honeysuckle Cottage. The three women surveyed with curiosity a lady with greying hair who stepped out of the vehicle and proceeded up the path before vanishing from their sight through the front door.

"Who's that?" asked Beth.

"No idea, I don't recognise the car either," replied Josie, as the children clambered into Beth's Range Rover.

"Josie, you and Max must come to dinner at Lime House one Sunday," Kate began before lowering her voice, "and if I can help in anyway, I mean, spiritually, then give me a ring."

"Thank you Kate, I might do that."

With the children waving frantically from the rear seat window, Josie watched as the four by four made its way down the lane.

Back in her cottage, she was just filling the dishwasher when the doorbell rang. Looking through the spy hole, she immediately recognised the face standing outside; it was the lady in the red Honda.

CHAPTER 23 – AN UNFINISHED TALE

The stranger met Josie's gaze with an uneasy air the minute she opened the door. She was a very smartly dressed woman in a navy dress and jacket, and her hair, cut short, framed her delicately featured face perfectly.

"Mrs. Forrester? I'm sorry to disturb you, but I'm the owner of Honeysuckle Cottage. I wondered if you had a minute, whether I could come in for a chat?"

"Yes, of course, please come in – the place is a bit of a mess, I'm afraid; I haven't had time to clean up after my visitors."

Josie led her into the front room and they sat down on facing chairs in front of the inglenook fireplace. There was an awkward silence before the woman suddenly sprang to her feet.

"It was such a shock, hearing about Pat's death; I really can't believe she's gone. I understand you found her body, Mrs. Forrester?"

Josie was immediately concerned and felt somewhat uncomfortable about the woman's obvious distress.

"Yes – I wasn't on my own, though; the doctor was with me when we found her. Was Pat a personal friend of yours?"

The woman's eyes had a look of panic about them, and she started pacing back and forth across the carpet, clasping her hands together, fighting with whatever it was that was troubling her.

"I'm staying with my husband at The Bull, it's

quite comfortable there, very old-fashioned, but we like that."

"Good. Look, was there something particular you wanted to talk to me about, only I don't want to rush you but ..."

The woman finally re-took her seat. "We've been at the police station answering their questions. I'm sorry. I'm very upset. Pat ... well, she meant the world to me, you see."

Josie sat forward and spoke softly. "The police have talked to me, too, there's still a question about her death; they told me they're not ruling anyone or anything out at the moment, if that's what's worrying you."

"No, no, you don't understand. Pat wrote to me before she died. I didn't receive the letter until yesterday – bloody post. I had no choice but to hand it into the police, so now they know."

"Now they know what?" asked Josie.

She jumped to her feet again and moved towards the window. "I shouldn't have said anything, forget I said that. Oh, I'm so shaken up by this whole matter."

"Would you like a drink, some brandy perhaps?"

"Yes, thank you, I'm not usually like this. My husband doesn't know I'm here; he would have insisted he came with me if he knew – he thinks I just popped to the shops."

Josie poured her out a small glass of brandy and handed it to her. She was beginning to think that perhaps she shouldn't have let this stranger into her cottage. She glanced up at the clock; it would be at least an hour before Max got home.

Finally sitting down again, the woman took a sip from her glass. "I can see by your face you think I'm quite mad, but I can assure you I'm not. Look, the reason I'm here is because Pat also sent me the manuscript of the book she was writing and I understand you have a copy?"

"Yes, I do, she gave it to me on the last day I saw her."

"Have you managed to read it?"

"Yes I have, although I don't think she had quite finished it – but that's not going to happen now, is it?"

"No … she's no longer here to finish it, but I am – I know how the story ends you see …" A look of complete surprise erupted across Josie's face. "I'm sorry, I should have introduced myself … my name's Mrs. Maddox, Mrs. Mary Maddox."

Josie gasped and fell back in her chair. "You're Mary, the Mary in the book?"

"Yes, and, as you can see, I survived. I've come here to tell you in my own words what happened after the gun went off – if you want me to, that is?"

"Are you saying it was a true story?"

"Most of it, well, the bare bones are there anyway."

Mary smiled, albeit nervously, for the first time since she had entered Brook Cottage. Josie's head was in a whirl. She could not believe she was sitting opposite Mary Macey, who over forty years earlier had fled from her fiancé to America.

"I honestly believe Cassey saved my life that day," Mary began. "She knew Diana's gun was in the drawer of the desk and when Joe attacked me she grabbed it and fired a shot into his leg. God, there was blood everywhere; she must have hit an artery or something. We were both screaming and crying and he was rolling around in agony. Nevertheless, we realised we couldn't stay around – we had to get away from him – so we fled from the house and made our way towards the beach. Of course, there was no one about, but we didn't know what else to do, we were so desperate. It was really eerie running along the sand with the roar of the waves in our ears and it was so dark – I know that sounds bizarre as it was night time, but there was no moon and the sky was swathed in a blanket of grey clouds. When we reached the rocks, the natural boundary to the estate, somehow we managed to climb over them, cutting our hands and legs as we did so. It seemed that we were running forever, but we reached the road eventually and flagged down a car. I remember the driver's face as he took one look at us, covered in blood; I half thought he was going to drive off again, thankfully he didn't. Anyway, he drove us to the police station and they sent out an ambulance and several police cars to Fouracres. They had to ram the gates to get in, but luckily they found Joe still alive. Apparently, he had managed to crawl into the hall and was crying for his mother … Sorry, could I have a glass of water? My throat's very dry."

Josie went into the kitchen and poured them both a glass of water and added a little bit of whiskey to hers.

"Thank you," said Mary, taking the class from Josie's hand. "It was a terrible time. Joe was arrested at the scene and from there he was taken to a secure unit at the hospital. It was over a year before he came to trial. In the meantime I flew back home, economy class this time!"

"I see, so you and Steve, how … I mean, you

obviously got married."

Mary grinned. "Yes, eventually we did. My poor dad was there to meet me at the airport with my brother Edward. I felt dreadful that I had put them through so much worry. Steve came round the next day and I refused to see him at first, but dad said I should listen to what he had to say. Apparently, on the evening of our engagement party, he had passed out in our hotel bed and the next thing he was aware of was the sound of me screaming out his name and Violet's face looking down at him, before he passed out again."

"So, you forgave Steve and you got back together?"

"Not immediately, it was all still very raw. I never saw Violet again though; I heard she went back to her job on the cruise ship and, as far as I know, married a sailor."

"Probably the best thing, she didn't turn out to be much of a friend, did she? Did you have to go back to America for Joe's trial?"

"Yes, this time Dad, Edward and Steve came along too. It was truly awful to see Joe in the dock. His lawyer put forward a plea of insanity as a result of his mother's death. How his grief from her passing had not been recognised by doctors; that if they had picked up on it and he had been given the counselling he so obviously needed, then, well, his life might have turned out quite differently. Of course, his journal played a big part in his conviction; it was all there you see, written in his own hand. In the end, he was sentenced to life imprisonment, without any possibility of being released. I remember clearly the day he was sent down, the look on his face as he screamed out to Cassey how she had betrayed him. The poor girl was beside herself. I always found it weird though that he didn't blame me for his arrest; only Cassey. After the trial, we flew back home and our lives resumed. I married Steve the following year and together we moved into a small flat. My aunt never did go back to her cottage and, when she finally died, she left it to me in her will."

"Oh my goodness, are you telling me Honeysuckle Cottage used to belong to Alice Macey?"

"Yes, that's right, she must have lived here before you moved to Willow Green?"

"You're right, we didn't move here until the eighties. It's surprising though that you and I have never met up until now. So what happened to Cassey?"

Mary stared at me for a long time. "Cassey felt she didn't want to live in Florida anymore and wrote to me to ask if she could visit. Well, that visit, as it turns out, lasted for the rest of her life."

Josie's eyes began to fill with tears. "Are you saying what I think you're saying: was Pat, Cassey?"

"Yes … Pat Wood was Cassey Ellis, strangely I never knew her surname until the trial. She lived near us for a while and worked with me in the bakery. We would chat about the past, that's how she knew so much about my family and me and was able to put so much detail in her book. She had not lived in England long before she met and married a long distance lorry driver, Donald Wood. He was a real bastard to her; if you believed the gossip, he had relationships with women all around the country. Their marriage, understandably, only lasted a couple of years before she divorced him. She had already changed her name to Pat Smith when she decided to stay in England because she was frightened that Joe, even from his prison cell, would find her and somehow take his revenge, so when she married, it changed again and she became Mrs. Pat Wood."

"Poor woman, living in fear all those years, I wish I had known about her torment."

"She didn't want anyone to know, Josie – I hope I can call you Josie?" Josie smiled sweetly and nodded. "She didn't want anyone to know because it was another life, as far as she was concerned. Nevertheless, it did play on her mind and writing this book I guess was a kind of therapy; she wanted the world to know that Joe was not the monster portrayed in the media. She really did love him, even after everything that had happened. Anyway, now you've heard the ending, can I ask you to destroy your copy of the manuscript and I will destroy mine, so our story will end here. To be honest, I don't want my children and grandchildren reading about my past; I'm not exactly proud of it."

"If that's what you want me to do, then that's what I'll do," said Josie.

"By the way, the funeral will be in two weeks' time and I'll be back here then with the rest of the family, so we'll be able meet up again." Mary moved into the hall before turning and taking Josie's hand in hers. "Thank you for being a good neighbour to my friend Cassey; I know she thought the world of all of you."

Mary Maddox climbed into her car and drove away. Everyone, thought Josie, has secrets, some obviously more intriguing than others.

THE FINAL PART

CHAPTER 24 – WITHIN THESE WALLS

Joe Carter folded the old newspaper cutting and placed it under his mattress. What a find, after all these years. It was the beginning of another day, another week and another month of continued confinement in the Pensacola prison, a more congenial establishment than his former residence, from where he had been moved almost ten years previously. He had earned his place by becoming a model prisoner and now he was no longer considered a danger to society. His lawyers were still hopeful of getting him released one day, however Joe was realistic and believed the slimy devils were giving him false hope and simply wanted his money.

He winced as he dressed, fighting the pain in his joints that old age had decided to bestow on him. He shuffled through the yard towards the building housing his studio. Oh yes, he had been allowed to continue with his photography, thanks to his psychiatrist, who had advised the prison authority that, for his mental state, it would be a good idea to keep him occupied with something he enjoyed doing – after all, this place was more than likely his final home. His photographic work, producing calendars and wall art, created within the confines of the prison, had helped over the years to raise money to fight breast cancer, a charity naturally very dear to him. He hoped his mother Diana, from her seat in heaven, would find it in her heart to be proud of him, even after all the bad things he had done.

At night, his dreams were now of Fouracres, riding Cheyenne along the white sandy beach with the sound of the breaking waves and the sun beating down relentlessly on his back. However, his former home no longer existed; bulldozers had come in and flattened the area soon after he had been sentenced and, rising like a phoenix from the ashes, a Carter hotel stood in its place – a fitting monument to its deceased owner, Frank Carter.

There was a small package waiting for him on his workbench when he arrived in his studio and he knew exactly what it contained. He had anticipated, after all these years, with the changes of management and staff, that no one had been bothered to read his personnel file lately, about how he had carried out his killings; how he had used cyanide from developing chemicals to murder his first three victims.

He held up one of the bottles of developing fluid and the minute the warden diverted his eyes, he slipped it into his jacket pocket. Now he had everything he needed. Later, back in his cell, he brought out the box of chocolates he had purchased the day before. He recalled the ribbing he had received from the other inmates when they caught sight of him carrying the red heart-shaped box back to his cell. *"Joe's got a girlfriend,"* and *"give her one for me, Joe."* It went on and on, but he ignored the lot of them.

Carefully, he filled the syringe he had stolen from the medical centre with the fluid and began injecting the chocolates, before resealing the box and wrapping it up ready to send.

Removing the crumpled newspaper article once more from beneath his mattress, he sat down on his bed and read it again.

The brutal murder of Doctor Daniels has shocked the inhabitants of Willow Green, a sleepy village that lies in the heart of Hampshire. Our reporter has been speaking to villagers and everyone has had only good things to say about him. Mrs. Patricia Wood, pictured here by the picturesque village green …

He had recognised Cassey almost at once, even after such a long time. Yes, she was obviously older, nevertheless, it was the mole on her cheek (he recalled she always called it her beauty spot) and her eyes that gave her away – he was always very fond of those big chestnut eyes. The newspaper had been used to pack out a handful of books sent to an inmate from his British girlfriend; they had been laying in storage for years, right under Joe's nose. It was not hard to find her address, thanks to the Internet. Now, with a stamp and a label, he popped the parcel in the post. He actually anticipated that when she saw the Florida postmark she would know it was from him and throw them away in the trash. Yes, he trusted she would not eat them and in reality he did not want her to. He just felt he had to send them, to let her know he knew she was still out there and he had not forgotten her betrayal.

He did not sleep well that night, tossing and turning in his bunk. Why the hell did he do it? Why did he send them? What was wrong with him? He had harboured hate for her all these years, for what she had done to him, but – if he were truly honest with himself – it was disappointment rather than hate, that someone he loved could destroy him. Christ, he loved her. Rising from his bed, he moved towards the cell door and started screaming for the guard, he had to tell someone about the parcel ...

***

Honeysuckle Cottage felt particularly cold when Pat returned from her visit to Josie, so to warm herself up she lit the fire. Reaching up to the mantelpiece, she lifted the clock from its prime position, opened the back, turned the key three times and then returned it to its rightful place before making her way into the kitchen to make a cup of tea. She thought again about her visit to Doctor O'Brien. He could be wrong; it would not be the first time a doctor had made the wrong diagnosis or a lab technician had muddled up the results. Ovarian cancer, shit. The pain in her side was getting worse, much worse; she swallowed two more of her prescribed tablets and waited for the agony to ease. Sometime later, opening the box of chocolates, she stared down at the little offerings. There was no card, but she knew they were from Joe; the Florida postmark was, in itself, a tell-tale sign. After all these years, how did he manage to find her? She caressed the box with her fingers, imagining how it would feel to touch the hand that had once touched the box, to look into his eyes again, to kiss the lips that she had never kissed. Oh god, she still loved him. She understood why he had sent them. She had let him down and he would never have forgotten that. She took out a pad and started to compose a letter to Mary.

My Dearest Mary, I trust you and your family are well. Sadly, my dear friend, I have some bad news. Yesterday, my doctor told me I am dying. It's too late for any treatment; the cancer has become too invasive. He said if only I'd gone earlier, but that doesn't help me now. Please don't be sad, my years here in Willow Green have been some of my happiest, with so many good friends and neighbours around me. I wanted you to know that today I heard from Joe. Yes, he found me; I always knew deep down he would. He sent me some chocolates; I would like to believe he remembered it's my birthday in a few weeks, but perhaps that's just wishful thinking. I want it to go on record that I do realise that his intention in sending them to me is probably not an honourable one. I betrayed him, Mary, all those years ago and he has never forgiven me and I have never forgiven myself. I will eat as many as I can. Mary, please don't hate him, I couldn't bear leaving this world knowing you hate him. Your friend forever, Cassey x

She folded the letter and slipped it into an envelope, which she addressed in her beautiful handwriting. Needing a stamp, she put on her coat and made her way towards the post office in the high street. Laura Cain, the postmistress, looked up and beamed as she always did as soon as she entered the shop.

"Afternoon Pat, what can I do for you today?"

"Just a first class stamp please, Laura." Taking the stamp from Laura's grasp, she gazed directly at her. "Thank you Laura, thank you for everything, you've always made me feel welcome in here and I appreciate that." Laura watched, with puzzled unease, as Pat made her way out of the shop, before turning to serve her next customer.

Walking home along the familiar cobbled side streets, Pat's face broke into a broad smile at seeing the school bus dropping off the local children and watched as they raced off eagerly towards their respective homes. It brought back fond memories of the times when she would look after Beth and Emma on the days when Josie was staying late at school because of parents' evening or rehearsals for a play. She found she was in her element then, cooking them their tea and listening to their chat about their school day. It was in those precious moments she wished her life had been more fulfilling and regretted not ever having children of her own.

Back in her little cottage, she went round each room and closed the curtains. Holding the box of chocolates firmly in her hand, she began to climb the stairs to her bedroom. She did not bother getting undressed, what was the point? She had always loved this room with the pink floral wallpaper, so it seemed fitting somehow that this is where she would take her last breath. She took one final look around her and said a little prayer, asking for forgiveness, before she began to place the chocolates between her lips. It was a horrible feeling, the choking before death. Nevertheless, as she moved into the next world, he was there, waiting to take her hand.

EPILOGUE

Willow Green Church was packed to the rafters as mourners gathered to show their last respects to a truly memorable village character. All her friends and neighbours were there, and even people she simply passed the time of day with in the street had come together to say their final farewells. In silence, the coffin was carried along the ancient aisle of the church, before coming to rest by the altar. The Reverend Stanton took his place in front of the congregation and gave his eulogy to a sweet lady, which was followed by a poem read by Beth, who broke down in tears as she delivered the last few words.

After the ceremony, everyone mingled for a while in the well-kept graveyard. Josie and Linda's families were talking quietly together when Josie suddenly nudged her friend.

"Don't look as if you're staring, but see that woman in the black lacy dress over there speaking to the Reverend? Well, that's Mary, you know, the one in the book, who owns Honeysuckle Cottage."

Linda put on her glasses and looked over in the Reverend's direction.

"Oh yes, I see, shall we go over? You can introduce me."

"Ok, but she doesn't know you read the book too, so please don't mention it."

"Of course not sweetie, my lips are sealed."

Mary greeted Josie and Linda warmly and promptly introduced her to her family, who, both women felt, they knew very well through the writing in Pat's manuscript. Steve, whose hair was now strikingly white, still had a little twinkle in his eye. Edward and his partner, both dressed in immaculately tailored black suits, seemed relaxed and happy. Lastly, Mary's dad, George, now a little old man in his eighties and confined to a wheelchair, shook the women warmly by the hand. After exchanging pleasantries, Josie and Linda made their way back to their own families.

"Well, that was a bit freaky," remarked Linda. "I must say her husband is still a very attractive man."

"Linda, really, you're a married woman," laughed Josie.

"By the way, I've been meaning to ask you, have you shredded the manuscript yet?"

Josie looked down at her feet. "No, not yet. There's something that's been bothering me about the whole thing. Why did Pat print two copies? I think it's because she knew Mary would be upset and want it destroyed; handing a copy to me, meant there was just a chance Joe's story might be published as she had intended. So, until I decide the best thing to do, I'm going to hold on to it."

"You're a little devil on the quiet, aren't you sweetie?" Linda linked arms with her best friend as they re-joined their families.

"We're going to the pub, Mum, are you coming?" asked Beth.

"I'll be along in a while, I just want to look at the flowers and have a quiet moment, if that's ok?"

"Just don't be too long, darling," said Max, leaning

in towards her and kissing her mouth softly.

***

The wreaths had been laid out in a neat row, a wonderful tribute, Josie thought, to a woman who was passionate about all things floral.

"They are beautiful, aren't they?" said a voice behind her. Josie turned around quickly and came face to face with DI Sam Adams. "I'm sorry, did I startle you?"

"I was just lost in thought. It was nice that you came, it was a wonderful service, wasn't it?"

"Yes, it was. Actually, I wanted a chance to speak to you. I understand Mrs. Maddox came to see you the other day?"

"Yes, she did and we had a nice chat."

"Good, well I thought you should know that Pat Wood died from eating chocolates laced with cyanide." Josie looked at her alarmed. "Apparently, she was aware she was already dying from cancer. We believe she knew who sent them and had guessed the sweets contained poison, but still ate them." Josie gasped at this news, as Sam continued, "Anyway, we traced the package: the box of chocolates came from a prison in Florida; they had been sent by a Joseph Carter, a Lifer, who Pat apparently used to work for."

"I see ..." said Josie, not totally surprised at this bit of information. "So, was it murder or suicide?"

"That's a good question. Pat wrote what we have interpreted as a suicide note before she died. So, I'm afraid, if she truly believed there was poison in the chocolates and she ate them willingly, then, well, it was suicide. Unfortunately, Joseph Carter died in his cell from a heart attack the day after he mailed the package, so he's no longer around to be interrogated. The guard who found him said that Mr. Carter had tried with his last breath to tell him something about a package, but he had passed away before he could give him any details. I'm guessing, maybe, he regretted sending it and wanted to warn her. I just thought you should know."

Josie stood in quiet contemplation, absorbing Sam's tragic words. So, it looked like Pat had taken her own life. To add to this heart-breaking tale, Joe must have cared for her after all – how truly sad it was that he never got the chance to tell her. They had lived apart for all those years but now, at least, Josie believed, they were together again.

"On a brighter note," Sam suddenly began, "well, I hope you think it's a brighter note, you will be having a new neighbour in a couple of weeks. I've just signed a six months tenancy agreement for Honeysuckle Cottage."

"Oh, great, yes, that's a surprise. I'll look forward to getting to know you better," replied Josie a little hesitantly, wondering how Max would react to having the police living next door, "mind, you might find us a bit quiet around here."

"I don't know, the village has definitely had its fair share of criminal activity in recent years, I'm pretty sure there will be more to investigate in the future and I'll be right there in the heart of it." She smiled warmly before walking away, leaving Josie, at last, alone in the graveyard.

Dark clouds were gathering overhead and a slight drizzle had started falling. Pulling her coat tightly around her, Josie stood before the final wreath of pale yellow and cream flowers. Turning over the condolence card, she felt a surge of emotion, as she digested the words sent by an old friend, it simply read: *'From one Angel to another x'*.

THANK YOU!

To my Reader:

Many thanks for buying *A Blackened Heart*, I hope you enjoyed reading it.

If you did enjoy it, please post a review at Amazon, Goodreads or your favourite social network site and let your friends know about *A Blackened Heart*.

Look out for the other books in the *Willow Green* series – *All For the Love of Josie* and *A Troubled Soul*.

More stories from *Willow Green* coming soon.

Happy Reading!
All the best
Evelyn

CONTACT DETAILS

Like on Facebook: facebook.com/1evelynharrison

Cover designed by: www.StunningBookCovers.com

Published by: Raven Crest Books
www.ravencrestbooks.com

Like us on Facebook:
facebook.com/ravencrestbooksclub